Dear Sandi —

This is the book I wanted to write for a long time. It is an allegory (introduction to the 12 Signs (Rays).

I hope you enjoy it — I hope you are well in these CRAZY times!

Best wishes,
Siorx

Cassandra's Tale

Invitation to the Circle

Sioux Rose

Copyright © 2008 by Sioux Rose.

COVER art by Carmen Day. Interior sketches by Share Tanzer!

ISBN:		Softcover		978-1-4257-8543-7

All rights reserved. No part of this book may be reproduced or transmitted in any form or by any means, electronic or mechanical, including photocopying, recording, or by any information storage and retrieval system, without permission in writing from the copyright owner.

This is a work of fiction. Names, characters, places and incidents either are the product of the author's imagination or are used fictitiously, and any resemblance to any actual persons, living or dead, events, or locales is entirely coincidental.

This book was printed in the United States of America.

To order additional copies of this book, contact:
Xlibris Corporation
1-888-795-4274
www.Xlibris.com
Orders@Xlibris.com

CONTENTS

What The Blink! 9
The Laboratory 18
The Elementals 25
Return To The Magic Spot 35
Final Preparations 41
Invitation To A Queen's Ball 48
Meeting The Twelve Rays 54
Showtime! 68
Peacemaking Forces 96
A Return To The Garden 101
A Parade Of Visitors 105
The Harvest 114
Homecoming 120
Ezekiel's Super Savvy Guide To Becoming Stellar Sign-Wise 129
Vocabulary List Supplemental Guide 133
Sioux Rose: The Author and Her Vision 145

DEDICATION

For the magicians, that see, know, and look more intently than the rest of us do. They urge us to open our senses! And for those that guide the great work of healing humanity's broken heart and wounded spirit down the long ages. Also for the children, a few within my circle: Bobby Black, Emily Good, Savanna Artigue, Dylan Webster, Stevie Merriman, Joseph & Daniel Maromarco, and my blessed new first grandson, Phoenix. With further consideration for our children's children: may we learn to live in peace to make their ways possible in this world. Lastly but hardly least, for these radiant members of the twelve rays who have shared my close and lasting friendship, often won my love.
They include:
From the first ray: Shari Eve Rosenberg, Aida Guzman, Molly Jubitz, Mark Newman, Shirley & Milton Firkser and Vincent Procida
From the second ray: Judit Child, Darlene Nash, Dennis Littleton, Lori Webster, Mario Carabarin, Arturo Molina, and in memory of Ron Lane and Ted Iseli
From the third ray: Rachel Nicole Fernandez, Estella Valles Acosta, Denei Horan, Nelson & Grace Wee, and in memory of Mary Procida
From the fourth ray: In memory of Frances Lear, Richard Clark, and Roberto Millian
From the fifth ray: Leslie Artigue, Lee Sloms, Millie Rivera, Diane Covan, and in memory of Sybil (and the Cybeles that came before her)
From the sixth ray: Bernice Rosenberg, Suzanne Schwedock, Fred McCreedy, Carol Christine, and Mirtha Castro
From the seventh ray: my late father Abraham Rosenberg, Gabrielle Alyssia Fernandez, Mary Prados, Axel Urbanic, and Alan Maltz,
From the eighth ray: Carlos Valdes, Robin Margolies, and Neil Reilly

From the ninth ray: James Caruso, Nanci Lynn Porter,
Bill Reed, Sandi Antonelli,
Wayne Ammons and Piquette Price
From the tenth ray: Lynn Knight, Sandra Schindler,
Manuel Casiano, Lewis Lapham,
Jorge Vega, and in memory of Mili Arango, and Grandma Becky
From the eleventh ray: Cynthia Civil, Robin Matthews,
Judi Rose Roth, Kevin Trudeau, Lynne Sallot, Nora Casiano,
Francisco Domenech, and in memory of Ron Weaver
From the twelfth ray: Anna Molina, Chaun Muir,
Ralph Nader, and Govind.

We all belong to the great circle!
And are continually born and reborn related to one another!

WHAT THE BLINK!

Perhaps Cassandra jumped ridiculously high because school was finally out and summer opened before her like a gateway to the unknown. She felt free! And what better place to begin vacation than right there on her backyard trampoline this warm June evening? Each lift propelled her higher. She fancied herself a great bird. "Who doesn't want to fly?" She mused to herself until the voice of caution came echoing by, "Cassandra! If you keep jumping like that you just might turn your brain into jellybeans!" She knew that was Mom's way of joking while also reminding her to be careful. Suddenly growing tired of the athletic challenge she set for herself, Cassandra gingerly climbed down from the trampoline while simultaneously noticing the backyard air suddenly alive with tiny bursts of pulsing light, inexplicable! Then she remembered it was the season of the fireflies, those delightful creatures that come fully equipped with their own taillights! Or something like that. One showed off boldly as it blinked its tiny beam right before her nose. "How do you do that?" she asked, not really expecting an answer. Like magic, the tiny flickering lights appeared and disappeared as if animated by a hidden musical source. There was indeed a rhythm to it. Clearly they were all intent on communicating in their own unique way. How she wished she could understand! The only way to tackle the answer was to confront the mystery head-on which Cassandra was quite prepared to do. Into the house she marched intent upon finding the perfect glass jar with a tightly fitting lid. That way she could observe the creatures up close and personal, and perhaps come to understand how they did what they did. Sure, she could turn on the computer and search the Internet, or grab a library book; but there was something far more compelling about learning the secret for herself. She just could not let the opportunity pass without acting fast! She was determined to discover how a firefly could turn on a light of its own. How could it do the seeming impossible?

In her evident enthusiasm Cassandra must have knocked a good many kitchen cabinets about; so naturally her mother appeared on the scene to check what all the commotion was about. Cassandra wasn't sure if her mother read her mind or surmised from the exquisite display of evening firelight what she was seeking; but the sought after jar quickly appeared in her mother's outstretched hand. As Mrs. Chambers watched her daughter scurry back into the yard, memories of her own childhood discoveries were rekindled. She certainly hoped she would not have to lecture Cassandra on the benefits of returning the creature to its proper environs after a brief observation period. She believed she had raised a daughter sensitive enough to come to that conclusion on her own.

Cassandra was not altogether sure if catching one firefly would prove adequate to her ad hoc research. Perhaps it would prefer its glass habitat in the company of a companion? She placed the jar on top of the trampoline and went about the yard cupping her hands until her strategy was honed and she caught one. The effort was somewhat hesitant as Cassandra was not altogether sure she could avoid a tiny electric shock in so doing! By this time darkness had fully descended and Cassandra heard her name called back into the house for wash-up and the inevitable bedtime routine. Merrily she ascended the stairs to her bedroom loft with jar and contents in hand. Her bedroom was a colorful world of its own with hanging mobiles that caught the morning sun. Each day they delicately reflected the light in alluring, sometimes enchanting patterns. Cassandra noted the details with pride and pleasure; after all, this was her room. She carefully placed the glass jar, firefly included, on the windowsill and laid out her toothbrush before covering it with her favorite mint paste. After giving her teeth a dedicated brushing, she realized that all the jumping had indeed made her sleepy; so after running downstairs to kiss her mother and father goodnight, she was ready for bed. Gazing across the room to her firefly companion, she wished it sweet dreams; and half wondered if her own might be altered by the creature's bright company? And soon to sleep went she. But alas, her reveries were interrupted by the ringing of the telephone, reverberating across the house with a will of its own. Although she could not hear the conversation, she could sense a certain anxiety rushing over her parents. She knew the phone call changed something around; but she would not hear the full implications until morning. Meanwhile as she tried to find her way back to sleep, her nightlight illumined the room to reveal the firefly. By then it was looking quite weary and inanimate as it clung to the side of the jar. Perhaps it was her imagination; but the creature appeared to be begging for its freedom. She wasn't sure what came over her, but she opened the window, then the jar, and set the firefly off into the night air and dreams of its own. By morning, she would have forgotten the loss.

At breakfast the next day Cassandra headed downstairs in her pajamas. It was a liberating thing not to have to get dressed as there was no school bus to hurriedly catch. On the other hand her father was unusually preoccupied. Mother poured his coffee as he looked over the paper, barely sharing a sentiment. Cassandra got the unmistakable feeling that something was being kept from her; but she didn't let on what she sensed. Sure enough, once her father was out the door en route to work Cassandra's mother sat down and looking deeply into her daughter's eyes asked, "Cassandra? How would you like to spend your summer vacation with your Grandfather?" Before allowing the child a chance to respond, she continued. "Last night we received an urgent telephone call that your father is needed at his company's research lab which is quite a distance from here. Since he will be gone for several weeks, he's asked that I join him; and I thought that would provide the perfect opportunity for you to spend some time with your old Gramps. I'm sure he'd love your company! And what a yard he has out there on all that land! Why Cassandra, you'll have more fireflies to contend with than there are jars to fill! By the way, what did you do with that firefly?"

The youngster patiently let her mother finish her discourse before answering. "I heard the phone ring so late. When it woke me up, I noticed the firefly looked so lonely that I had to let him or maybe it was a her go free."

Mrs. Chambers studied her pretty little daughter with amusement; then asked for her thoughts a second time. "So how do you feel about spending time at your Grandfather's house, since I must accompany your father on this business trip?"

Pausing for a moment, Cassandra looked up and said, "Mother how can I say what I think since I never spent any time with him before? Is there anyone to play with out there? Can I call my friends back home? Does he have a computer?" All those expressed considerations felt like a mouthful.

"I suppose we'll all just take it one step at a time, huh? But we will need to get to packing; so I'd like you to consider what you'd like to take along. You'll have to choose carefully. Select a few of your favorite games, toys and books; as I don't want Grandfather to see so many bags that he'll think you're permanently moving in!" Both laughed.

"When will I be going?" Cassandra asked with a hint of poignant concern.

"Well, I wanted to speak with you first. It's just a matter of cementing certain details with your Grandfather. It's best to just tell him when we're coming. I'm afraid he gets so carried away with his researches, he'll forget plans made too far in advance."

"Is he still doing all those scientific studies?"

"Wild horses couldn't cart him away from that, I'm sure. But don't you worry. There will be plenty of things to occupy your interest once you get there. That's a promise!" The two ladies finished their breakfast cereal and fresh Florida orange juice, before heading upstairs where the packing could begin!

Not the next day, but the following one, Cassandra was told the family would be leaving for her Grandfather's estate bright and early the next morning. It was a strange feeling indeed to lie in her bed wondering what time spent away would actually feel like. She wondered how much she might change. Past years when she returned to school after summer vacation she noticed that many of the boys grew tall as trees, and girls filled out, too. She sensed she was about to face an adventure; and so with her sense of curiosity in tow, she bravely prepared to meet what lay ahead.

On the morning of the family's departure, breakfast went by faster than a runaway locomotive. The three entered the car in no time. Cassandra buckled herself into the backseat with her favorite toy toucan, a gift she had kept since she could remember. Tuke was also buckled in right next to her. "Now I hope you brought something to read or otherwise occupy your mind, Cassandra," her father half-warned. "This is a very long trip. If there's not much traffic, we should get there in time for an early dinner." Mother had that all figured out, the contents already sending an alluring scent from the picnic basket she'd efficiently packed early that morning. Since its contents were mysteriously prepared the night before, Cassandra prayed that her Mom had included some tasty treats to sustain her across the long day's journey.

"You brought your *Alice* and *Harry Potter*, too, right?" Cassandra's mother inquired.

"Yes, mother," she answered while watching the car roll out of town to pass familiar sights. Her father's words coiled about in her mind. She wondered just exactly how anyone could occupy a mind? You could occupy a house, of course; or place a "for rent" sign up if not. She laughed quietly to herself. Maybe she would read a book? Yet the motion of the car interrupted the steady gaze of her eyes as they sought to follow each tiny line across the page. No, that would not work for Cassandra. Not now, anyway. She began to realize that getting to Grandfather's would itself be a relief! Yet it wasn't long before the family ventured outside their hometown and the road opened to more interesting sights. Suddenly Cassandra found her attention piqued by the scenery. A set of dark clouds loomed ahead and she wondered if their little car might come face to face with a real tornado? She imagined her suitcase opening to an angry swirling cloudburst with her panties raining down on some unsuspecting neighbor! That made her laugh out loud.

"What's so funny back there, Cassandra?" Her mother asked cheerfully.

"Nothing," Cassandra answered, not wanting her Dad to say she was talking nonsense. Maybe her mind was the type best occupied by imagination; but Dad's was a zone of a different sort. "It's probably going to be so boring at Grandfather's all summer," she thought aloud.

"Life is never boring when you open your mind to learn something new," her father offered with calm wisdom.

She gave his words some thought; and the process must have been a deep one, for it wasn't long before Cassandra fell into a nap. This made the time pass rapidly until at last she woke with a hardy yawn to ask, "Where are we now?" Her father answered, "It's not much further at this point. We're less than an hour away."

"Well how far have we gone then?" She asked to be sure.

"We've been traveling about four hours. You fell asleep two hundred miles back, young lady!" Just as the sky took on delicate colors of pink and orange, the family pulled up at the Professor's estate. "Take a look at all those weeds! My father has really let the place go!" Mrs. Chambers said these words with marked regret in her voice.

The observation led Mr. Chambers to the conclusion that Cassandra might well take advantage of the situation by making a tidy garden her summer's project and pursuit! "Looks like you've got your work cut out for you, my girl." He uttered.

Cassandra thought he was teasing. No sooner did the car wind its way down the long unpaved driveway to stop before a cozy looking cottage set far into the wilds, did Grandfather emerge right on cue. First he hugged his daughter, her Mom; then he shook her Dad's hand and gave him a rudimentary hug; and then he held his chubby arms out to embrace his delightful granddaughter who he'd not seen in some time. She jumped in and nearly knocked the old fellow over. "Sorry, Grandpa . . ."

He regained his balance, brushed himself off, and then noted the picnic basket that his daughter was retrieving from the car. "Great weather for a picnic! And it's a good thing; since I haven't the faintest notion what Cassandra likes to eat. We'll have to shop this week, won't we?" He said, looking straight at Cassandra.

"Dad, do you have a nice table cloth that we can put over your patio table?"

He looked about giving Cassandra the distinct impression that he was truly an absentminded professor, if ever there was one. But before he could answer the question, Cassandra's Mom took a colorful beach towel from the backseat of the car. Meanwhile Dad grabbed her suitcase, while she took Tuke into the house. Before being given an official tour of the place, she let herself inside to notice a colorful parrot staring at her as if he anticipated her arrival. "Can you talk?" She asked, coaxing the bird for a response. He remained mute, apparently sizing up the little girl before responding. "Okay, be like that if you want to. We're having a picnic. If you're nice, I'll bring you a treat." Those words did the trick because the bird called after her, "Okay. Okay." She liked that so much that she ran outside to tell her Mother what the bird had uttered, and left Tuke on a chair all alone inside!

Mrs. Chambers got out tasty sandwiches and a jar of apple juice kept chilled thanks to frozen freezer bags. "Oh, I just love dining outside. Don't you, Cassandra? There's really nothing quite like a picnic in the outdoors." But at the moment she uttered those words, the first of sundown's biting insects appeared and the diners found themselves swatting as much as biting.

"Pops, you'd probably have less of a bug problem out here if you took care of all this overgrowth," Cassandra's father stated authoritatively, only half hinting at how aggravating he thought the pest problem really was. The professor had a bit of a twinkle in his eye when he answered,

"Without pests there'd be no volunteers (he emphasized the word). Therefore I decided it would be counterintuitive to take out the underbrush."

Laughing, his daughter added supportively "You're absolutely right! How could your pesticide research progress without pests to test your concoctions upon?" As those words were exchanged, Cassandra began to wonder what she was getting into. In fact the adult conversation made her want to pursue the bird's further acquaintance. She hid a small pretzel as collateral for the creature.

"Grandpa, what's your parrot's name?"

"Ah. So you've already met Ezekiel, huh? Not much misses his eye. I named him Ezekiel. Not sure why, maybe a little bird gave me that idea." Everyone laughed.

"You mean Ezekiel who saw the wheel?" Cassandra remarked remembering the reference from a Bible story someone had read to her.

"One in the same; though I'm not sure if a wheel has anything to do with it." Everyone laughed again at the odd reference.

"So who's ready for desert?" Cassandra's Mother cooed. You could almost hear the smiles, as everyone reached over to taste the delectable brownies now displayed on the table. These would appear to have a short life expectancy given the enthusiasm of the crowd! Cassandra was so eager to bite into the long awaited chocolate treat that she haphazardly let numerous crumbs drop. Almost on cue, ants began to gather around the rich finds and cart them off to their doubtless nearby nest. No one seemed to notice. Nor did anyone happen to observe what might be taken for a family of roaches (more politely called Palmetto Bugs) just then making their way out of Cassandra's family car. Had anyone considered a close inspection, they might have further noted that each one of those creatures descended carrying its own small suitcase in tow! To the observant eye, more than one family reunion was evidently underway.

While everyone enjoyed desert, Cassandra's father did what fathers tend to do best. He began setting down some rules. "Now Cassandra, your Grandfather has graciously agreed to allow you to stay here for several weeks while I am away on a critical research project of my own. But he, too, is busy; so when he's involved in his lab research, you must respect that. It's my understanding that the lab is filled with a collection of acids and dangerous poisons, so it's no place for you to explore. Is that understood?" He asked with a tone that was more a command than a question.

"Yes, Father." The young girl dutifully responded.

"And while it's your Grandfather's express wish that we not remove the foliage that encourages the insects to make themselves of use to him in his researches; there certainly is no reason why you could not plant a small garden and apply yourself to a diligent and worthwhile summer project."

Again she responded, "Yes, Daddy." However she was secretly hoping to be excused from the table to learn what other words the bird might know. As the sky grew darker, and the bugs began to bite more persistently, Mr. Chambers gave his adoring wife that look that meant they best be getting on their way. He got up from the table, and Cassandra's Mother packed up the leftovers. Handing them over to Cassandra, she added, "See if you can find your Grandfather's fridge. You can snack on these tomorrow."

Cassandra ran inside and while she searched for the fridge, Ezekiel seemed to study her moves. Even though she spied the old fashioned machine through the doors that led to the kitchen, she asked the bird as if to deliberately test him: "Ezekiel. Hi, Ezekiel." She cooed, first. "Where is Grandfather's refrigerator, do you know?" She held up the pretzel treat as a lure. He waited until he'd nearly convinced her that he didn't have a clue before abruptly responding, "Straight ahead. Can't miss it!" Shocked at the bird's uncanny wit, she wondered if Grandfather had trained the creature to be so savvy; or if it was something that came to him naturally. It was that way with some kids at school, the ones who effortlessly confronted the most challenging schoolwork! In any case, she ran back outside, not wanting to cut the goodbye scene short. Since she would not be seeing her parents for some time she gave each one a huge hug and a double kiss for good luck. Then she stood outside and waved as the car passed down the long driveway. Only then did Cassandra notice the ants that had found their own picnic souvenirs not altogether accidentally left behind. The professor saw this and ran towards his laboratory, hurrying back with a red spray can. He began to spray and spray; but the insects, while looking groggy or half drunk still went about doing what they were already doing. "I knew I needed a higher dosage," he said to himself. "Let's get inside. It's only going to get worse out here. Besides, you'll no doubt want to see the room I fixed up for you. It used to belong to my cat, Mugsley. Quite a pal that cat, but I'm afraid he passed two years ago. You're not allergic to cats are you?" And before Cassandra nodded "No" the professor led the way. However at that very instant, the line of roaches that had made way from Cassandra's family car now entered the professor's home just in time for him to spy an unlucky one. With his trusty red can handy, the professor aimed his bug spray at the unfortunate creature. He became inordinately excited by the prospect of demolishing it! "Roaches! I detest roaches!" He said loudly while gaining upon the creature as it quickly sought refuge in a tiny hole behind the kitchen wall. "I'll get rid of these pests if it's the last thing I do!" He hollered and made himself so upset that sweat beaded up profusely on his forehead. He had to sit down and come to a complete stop just to compose himself after the ordeal.

"Grandfather: you shouldn't get so excited over bugs. They're just bugs!" And her wise counsel was followed by the no nonsense voice of Ezekiel offering an uninvited retort, "Quite right!"

"Ah shut up!" The professor touted back. Then noticing the look of bewilderment on his sweet granddaughter's face, he clarified. "I meant him," (pointing at the bird), "not you, my dear. Now, let me show you your room." He chuckled to himself, amused by the novel condition of sharing his home with his Granddaughter. Not having catered to a guest in quite some time, lest one consider the cat that had no doubt grown accustomed to his eccentricities living with the old fella so long, he was decidedly out of practice. He opened the door to a room that was rather dusty; yet it had a charming view of the abundant outdoor greenery. Old photos filled the walls, and a day bed boasted a worn but well crafted bedspread designed in an inviting white and yellow floral pattern. Cassandra determined in that singular instant that she could be quite comfortable in this new, well to her it was new, room. As she looked around Grandfather added, "We'll be sharing the bathroom. It's just down the hall. There is a fresh towel on the rack. Mine is the blue one, so you can use the red one. Okay? I suppose you'll want to freshen up before bedtime." She nodded, gave her Grandfather a hug; and then opened her little cosmetic bag, the tiny twin to the one her mother prized. Out came the toothbrush and off went Cassandra to face her familiar image in an altogether novel mirror. Would she appear exactly as she had previously beheld herself by summer's end? Or would she note any changes? She wondered; for indeed she had entered a very different world.

Her reverie was interrupted when the Professor called out, "If you wake later than seven, my dear, you may find that I am already at work in my laboratory. So just fix yourself a bowl of cereal, and pour yourself some juice. Things can be found in their logical places. Just look around, make yourself familiar, and help yourself. I generally break for lunch. So I'll see you then. Perhaps we'll go into town for a little shopping later, eh?"

"Sounds great, Grandpa." She squealed back, beginning to see the possibilities she had not quite considered before arriving in this new domain. From the vantage point of her makeshift bedroom, Cassandra could peer out the window into a night sky unimpeded by city or neighborhood lights. So many stars. They looked just like the fireflies, except for the fact that they didn't blink, or not as quickly as fireflies did, anyway. That was the last thought in her head before dreams carried her to yet another land.

THE LABORATORY

The shade of old oak trees obscured the morning sun. Thus when Cassandra naturally awakened she had no idea what time it was. Marching about the unfamiliar cottage in her pajamas, she came upon (as anyone might have guessed) a grandfather clock. It was almost nine! She washed up, grabbed Tuke, and then peeked into the kitchen; but there was not a sound to be heard. A note, however, was waiting for her on the refrigerator door instructing her to help herself to cereal. Grandfather had no doubt resumed his daily routine in his private laboratory. As she oriented herself to a new set of protocols (for at home, mother always prepared breakfast), Cassandra completely forgot about Ezekiel. In contrast he kept a close watch on her. Finally she broke the silence. "Good morning, Ezekiel. And how did you sleep?" Still expecting the standard "Polly wanna cracker" response, she was taken aback when the bird responded, "I've had better dreams. I'm afraid." Meanwhile Cassandra opened and closed cabinets in pursuit of a clean bowl and matching spoon. She'd found the cereal and the milk all right, and woke with a bona fide country breakfast appetite! Once in possession of the necessary objects, she sat down and began to eat the cereal as Ezekiel staggered back and forth in his cage, balancing his weight upon a singular bar. It seemed the wily bird was waiting for the right moment to offer his proposal. He patiently contemplated his approach as the young girl savored the granola. Her enthusiasm for the simple meal was revealed in every audible crunch. When finished, she quickly got up and began rinsing her dish which brought her quite close to Ezekiel's cage.

"Suppose you'll want to look around today to become familiar with your Grandfather's property?" She half-expected the bird to utter Grandfather's unusual name; but was truly glad that he did not. If the truth be told, she was relieved that Macaronius was the name inherited on her mother's side. Luckily, her father's surname was Chambers. It might be one thing for a person of the older generation to carry a name like Erroneous Macaronius; but no thanks. Cassandra Chambers was perfect for her! Lost in her own musings, she temporarily forgot to answer the bird's perfectly reasonable question. Instead she chose to adjust Tuke, who had slumped over from his kitchen chair perch.

"Yes. That sounds like a lovely thing to do." She responded after the delay.

"Well, you don't want to go off by yourself, do you, when I could show you things you would otherwise miss? Better a private tour with an experienced guide. And I recommend that you leave that thing (he meant Tuke) behind." With those words, Ezekiel used his long beak to pick at the lock on the birdcage. Long practiced in the failed art of escape he knew it would not budge; but how else to alert Cassandra to the fact that he needed a bit of assistance? Her response was one of puzzlement, until he said, "The key can be found on the shelf above the kitchen sink."

Cassandra looked the bird over like a detective scrutinizing the motives of a seasoned detainee. Then she conceded and dragged her chair over to the sink. From its height she could reach the indicated shelf. As her hand fished around in search of the key, Ezekiel's movements across the cage-bar grew more animated.

"I've been stuck in this dungeon, too long!" He uttered. "It would do us both good to get out for some fresh air!"

Cassandra fit the odd shaped key into the lock poised on the birdcage, and off it came. With the caution that results from never having tried something before, she gingerly put out her hand. Ezekiel wobbled; then climbed from her wrist to her shoulder where he seemed quite comfy. "Well, then. Let's get to it! Let the adventure begin!" The bird spoke with unmistakable enthusiasm as Cassandra led the two out the front cottage door. They walked towards the backyard table where the family picnic had recently transpired.

"Will you take a look at that! Nutra and Tidy-up. Why they never waste a minute!" The bird exclaimed as he looked down at the ground.

"I'm afraid I haven't the faintest idea who or what you are talking about?" She scolded.

"Quite right. That's because you haven't met them yet. I forget that it's impolite of me to presume that you would naturally share a bird's eye view of the world."

"Does Grandfather have any idea that you talk as much as you do?"

"If he and his scientific theorems are thoroughly convinced that birds can only repeat a limited repertoire, who am I to challenge the old boy this late in the game? Besides, preconceived notions do not allow themselves to be easily shattered by something as radical as a novel idea!"

Cassandra could not help but laugh when the bird put it so irreverently. "So will you tell me about Nutra and Tidy-up? I don't have any theories!" She added humorously.

"They are masters of detail and nuance; probably invented the first list. I am referring to those little ants right by your feet, dear lady. Cordially referred to as the sixth ray in nature's parlance. Nary a creature works harder."

"You have a good vocabulary for a bird! Now if you would be so kind as to tell me what is meant by nature's parlance?" She repeated the new words tentatively.

"Language. Every creature has a language. The trick is to still your mind long enough to attune to it. But that's another day's lesson. We have much to see! On with it then!" He sounded more like a commanding pirate than the bird atop its shoulder, as he urged Cassandra's footsteps onward across the overgrown property.

"Do you have any snakes out here? Or alligators?"

"Well, I confess I've been inside so long, it's been ages since I've seen either. But it's a fair guess that such creatures would make their homes in an unspoiled wilderness like this. Wouldn't you? That is to say if you were a snake or alligator. After all, there's not much room left for them these days, what with the human population growing so fast, moving about, converting swamp into shopping centers, parking lots, and so forth."

"You're very smart for a bird," she answered.

"Indeed." He responded immodestly just as they came to the door leading into the professor's private laboratory. Its warning was unmistakable. The foreboding skull and crossbones, universal symbol for dangerous poison was clearly posted at the entrance. Cassandra knew better than to disturb Grandfather in his researches. Ever since she was a little girl she recalled tales of his long and distinguished career as an entomologist. And although he was now officially retired, he was not unlike the legendary Scotland Yard detective Sherlock Holmes who remained ever in pursuit of the world's most cunning criminal mind, Moriarti. In a parallel fashion Grandfather would never relinquish his quest for the globe's most lethal pesticide. For him there was no greater criminal threat than that of insect pests; and he was determined to discover a remedy guaranteed to wipe them all out once and for all! On his large private property he was free to pursue this passionate ambition without any interruptions. And since Cassandra's visit was not planned in any formal sense, she was quite content to respect his need for private study. Thus the two passed the lab and left Erroneous to his chemical contemplations.

Continuing on their walk, the bird posed the following improbable question: "Have you ever gone on an official feather hunt?"

"A feather hunt? I thought you were going to say a treasure hunt!"

"Ah, but there are treasures to be found. That will come later I assure you; but for now, I think you might find yourself rather amazed with these remarkable objects. Feathers are wondrous things. And when they fall, like bits of magic displaying an astounding range of colors and camouflage, they hail from worlds where winged beings, perhaps the very angels, claim dominion."

That was a lot for a young mind to take in. Recognizing the mechanical difficulty in stooping down to check the ground for feathers, lifting a leaf here or there with a hefty bird on her shoulder, Cassandra extended her arm its full length, thereby guiding Ezekiel to a strong, steady branch. "Wait there. Let me see if I can find one."

"Not one!" He wryly corrected. "Why out here you're apt to find yourself blessed with the stunning aqua feather of the blue jay, the riveting crimson blade of the male cardinal, the symmetrically striped plume of the hawk, or the long imperial feather of yet another majestic bird of prey, the osprey."

As she looked around the wooded walkway, she suddenly took note of what she was doing. "I've never been on a feather hunt before. This is fun! I thought there'd be nothing to do at Grandfather's house!"

"This is just the beginning, Cassandra. Tomorrow we'll begin official classes."

"Classes! Not now! I just finished school!" She protested.

"Well, my dear, in point of fact the real school exists out here!" He made his case by aiming the full expanse of his wing at the natural panorama that lay before them. "I am quite sure you will find this a very different education. Elemental, as you shall see. I mean, what do you really know about the world? Have you taken any time to explore it? Made any discoveries lately? Or do you think such matters are best left to scientists like your Grandfather, all boarded up in his laboratory, as if it were a cave!"

Upon hearing those words, or possibly as a strategy to ignore them, Cassandra knelt down to spy a closer look at a sparking blue tendril as it peered out from under a clump of fallen leaves. "Look! Look what I found!" She held up the bounty for Ezekiel's perusal.

"Yes! That's it, that grand feeling of discovery. The first taste of it with more to follow! For learning what you don't yet know IS the greatest adventure of all. And I assure you it's not something to be missed!"

With those words, Cassandra bent over to give the bird a kiss, right on his crown. Although hard to prove, Ezekiel blushed under his cloak of bright blue, green and red feathers. He then climbed back to his favorite shoulder perch; and the two walked on further until they came to the property line, as evidenced by a fence with a padlock anchored into its singular and nearly ancient yet sturdy door.

"I think we've gone far enough for today. But the thing I want you to remember is this: you have come upon the greatest show on earth! Right here in your own, or shall we say, your Grandfather's own backyard!"

All that discovery made Cassandra hungry. Indeed, the sun was now nearly overhead. She remembered that meant it was high noon. Soon the afternoon atmosphere would quickly heat up and she was already impossibly thirsty. Ezekiel was right. It was time to head back to the house. The pair had essentially circled the property; and on their return route they came upon an old hammock worn from the changing weather conditions of northern Florida. Cassandra couldn't resist getting into it, which posed some serious balance problems for Ezekiel. He quickly made use of his long claws to grip the weave of the thing, while Cassandra rocked herself to see what it felt like. When she laid her head down, she noticed a trail of ants in exact linear formation marching beneath the hammock.

"No one works harder. Honestly. I've never known Nutra or Tidy-up to take a day off, not to mention a vacation." Now Cassandra recognized the ones Ezekiel was referring to.

"How do they always find their way to picnics? Whenever I drop morsels the ants find them before they even hit the ground!"

"Quite right there, my girl! The bird replied. "They are mindful masters of efficiency. Besides, Nutra can tell you anything you want to know, or perhaps would rather not know, about the constituents in the foods you eat and drink. Right, Nutra?" Ezekiel directed that comment right at the tiny ant who appeared to nod; but then again, Cassandra wondered if she was only imagining its response. Suddenly she remembered that Grandfather instructed that he took a break from his laboratory for lunch hour. They'd best get back inside quickly! By this time she had built up something of a sweat, and wondered what Grandfather would think if she showed up in disarray, no less with his caged bird loose atop her shoulder! She hoped she could beat him to the house, and safely restore Ezekiel to his appointed confines.

The two made haste for the cottage door; and no sooner did they enter, and Cassandra deftly place Ezekiel back in his lodgings, did the professor enter from a side door she had not yet noticed. She didn't even have time to secure the cage lock. She hoped Grandfather would not notice. He was in a very animated mood. It was rare for him to entertain although he had a friend or two who occasionally stopped by as she would soon find out. Right now he was taken in by his Granddaughter's delightful company and the business of the moment was lunch! The professor reached under the sink to grab a bottle of soap. This was not your everyday variety of cleanser. No, not at all! The professor's soap had to cut through whatever residue of poison clung to his chubby fingers. Even though he made every effort to maintain sanitary lab conditions, and protect his skin from exposure with rubber gloves, one could not be too careful when conducting such perilous research!

The professor was a short, stout man. Unbeknownst to Cassandra, Ezekiel had acquired a pet name for him: Shorty Portimer. A large mustache distinguished the professor's face and provided it with character, albeit the character of a cartoon figure! He was likable. Even his bald spot invited the proverbial pat on the head. Erroneous was also essentially good-natured; however, he could become quite serious when the occasion, such as that of his studies, called for it. After he assured himself that his hands were scrupulously clean, he began mucking about in search of spaghetti sauce. Varied shapes and sizes of pasta served as his favorite lunch. Cassandra stood close by as he filled a pot with water, then periodically checked his watch. The scientific mind preferred to accurately anticipate how much time was needed for water to boil; so the professor checked the experiment to make sure it was true to form and method. Cassandra quickly recognized that her grandfather was a lot more interesting to study than whatever it was that he was studying. When the water boiled, he emptied in some squiggly pasta of varied hues; and then scurried over to the pantry to obtain a glass jar of tomato sauce. Just when she thought he was stuck in scientific seriousness he began to sing a little ditty as he stirred the sauce. It went like this:

> "Delicious, Delocius, konnitius, konnotious
> Delicious, Delocious, konnitius, konnotious
> They'll never detect, they'll never tell
> When they ingest my chemical spell . . ."
> Alas when it's ready, all will be well . . .

Suddenly noting the child he forgot was there staring at him incredulously, he became visibly shaken with embarrassment.

"Oh, Cassandra, I lost track of you there for a minute. Excuse me. I got carried away. That's the song I like to use to inspire my research. It lifts my morale, and reminds me that I'm closer than I think to at long last coming upon the world's most invincible pesticide! It's just a tad embarrassing when someone else happens to hear my private tune. The fact of the matter is: I'm just not used to having company when I work!"

"Well, Grandfather, I just hope you never lose track and mix your chemical spell into our spaghetti sauce!" And with those words of wisdom, the two laughed heartily before enjoying their rather tasty lunch. They got along splendidly when they spent time together. Cassandra enjoyed his company, and recognized that she had likely inherited her distinctive curiosity streak from her Grandfather. However it would be several days before she would again find herself privileged with another one of Ezekiel's unusual guided tours. Strong rains had come to delay the promised classes! She was too polite to convey her sense of relief to Ezekiel. Given that she was restricted to indoor living until the wet weather passed over, she busied herself with items brought from home. She was well prepared as she had an assortment of coloring books and stories to read. She even tried her hand at sketching the shapes of trees as pretty as postcards just outside the cottage windows. Each room offered its own special view. She mostly forgot about Tuke, too. A real bird had come to replace him, and this one's conversation went well beyond what any pull string toy could ever deliver!

THE ELEMENTALS

On the fourth morning of Cassandra's summer adventure, the sun blazed with renewed assertion throughout the kitchen as she went about her morning routine. Ezekiel exuded an uncustomary silence that felt almost ominous. It left Cassandra with the comforting delusion that she might be off the hook with respect to the mandatory summer education program he had enthusiastically designed. The merry youngster sat down to crunch vehemently into her favorite cereal when the stillness was broken by a pensive parrot given to philosophical musings.

"By all means fill-up, for as the bright sun portends, today is the right time to begin those classes you so look forward to." As Cassandra took in the message, deliberating on an honest, albeit polite response of decline, the bird continued. "Were history's great explorers to look as glum as you, I declare there'd be no grand settlements in this, for some, new world. Let it be understood from the onset that the teacher is often as inspired by his students as vice versa. Thus enthusiasm, child! Let me see it begin with your smile!"

Cassandra did not mean to offend the bird, but caution was something of a habit she'd adapted in living her life thus far. Of course with only eleven years of conditioning, arguably there was available room for adaptation. Her face opened like the dawn into a sunburst and the smile portrayed was hardly a counterfeit. That bird had an uncanny way of getting to her. Besides, there were far less interesting companions than this one. She elected to place skepticism aside, and allow the wise bird to lead her. If there was something valuable to be learned, why would she stand in her own way?

Cassandra rose to dutifully wash her cereal bowl, cup, and spoon as Ezekiel looked her over.

"I'm afraid you'll need to change your attire, dear girl. Yesterday's rains have no doubt left just enough pond water for mosquitoes to proliferate. Pants and socks will cover your lower portions to ward off those buggers.

And a light shirt with long sleeves is also advisable." She laughed at the bird's choice of words, but sensed he was right. No one in their right mind would fancy becoming a banquet for bloodsuckers.

With lightning-like speed, Cassandra returned in a flash boasting her own ensemble of safari pants, light sweatshirt, heavy socks, and tacky sneakers.

"Goodness, girl! You do know how to make haste when the spirit seizes you!" In point of fact, Cassandra was tired of being cooped up inside, and grateful to get out and explore. Since she had deftly seized a strategic moment to return the lock to Ezekiel's cage to ensure that Grandfather would suspect nothing of their private outings; she was now intent to perfect the drill down to a virtual science! She slid a chair to the sink, grabbed the little key, and again released Ezekiel to the liberating outdoors. He climbed diligently up her extended little arm, and out the front door went the unlikely pair into the foliage-covered yard. This time they would not stop at the back gate. However, their progress was interrupted when something sticky and unwarranted caked across Cassandra's face and Ezekiel's left wing.

"Yuck! What was that?" She moaned and added with nothing short of impatient disgust.

"I half-apologize," said the amused bird, as he used his beak to filter off the detritus that had covered the two, courtesy of a well engineered and ingeniously secured spider web set between trees, not visible to either at their angle of approach. Of course neither Ezekiel nor Cassandra was the intended captive the net set by a clever creature sought to ensnare; nor would its owner be particularly thrilled to find its efforts upended before any coveted booty could be garnered from said labors. "C'est la vie," said the parrot practicing his best laissez faire French, as the precocious youngster came to the obvious conclusion that they had indeed walked through an enormous spider web.

"Maybe I should be your guide!" The child said in mock protest, not amused by the encounter. Of course what she didn't notice (nor did Ezekiel feel especially anxious to bring it her attention) was the large banana leaf spider standing by. Determined not to have lost all for its quite considerable threaded efforts, one of its eight legs slowly and surreptitiously extended to grasp the pretty pink ribbon attached to Cassandra's ponytail just as she passed under the remainder of the existing web.

"A souvenir" said the spider in a voice inaudible to Cassandra. Ezekiel heard it, and offered a perfunctory wink in return.

"Let us continue," said the bird, wishing to advance into an ambiance conducive to the intended lessons of the day. However, once again, their progress was impeded, this time by a long line of small, but potent fire ants.

Cassandra knew that the tiniest bite from one of these packed a painful punch. It was a memory that left wisdom in its wake; and so the two chose their path away from the march of the fire ant's army. Still, Cassandra could not help spying what looked to be an organized calisthenics formation among the creatures. Many were doing push-ups. To the naked eye it suggested the equivalent of human soldiers preparing for warfare at some kind of boot camp! She was astounded; and that was without even hearing their captain yell, "All right men! Prepare to pillage and plunder!"

Next they came upon a hefty beetle (later Cassandra would find in one of Grandfather's books a full explanation of these earth-moving creatures along with their given name: The American burying beetle). The pair stopped momentarily to observe the creature's studied movements. Cassandra recognized how much the beetle appeared to do exactly what farm equipment and bulldozers do. The specie had ingeniously adapted its own means for moving earth about. Ezekiel seemed to sense what she was thinking and uttered the following, "Often you will find that it is one of nature's own that makes a discovery and adapts it, only to be followed by some scientist or engineer claiming credit for accomplishing the work. And the reason why? Because this is the greatest laboratory on earth! Here trial and error has gone on for eons! As a result a great many inventions have been devised. I just thought I'd allot credit to where and to whom it's justly due!"

Cassandra considered that Ezekiel might be something of a magician, using the art of smoke and mirrors to divert her attention from where it was needed. Or was it rather that the high number of odd diversions side-tracked her ordinary thought process so much that she hardly noticed that the parrot was guiding them both to the property line where a fence waited to buttress any further efforts in pursuit of uncharted territory. Why would he head there? Its gate was obviously locked, and probably for a good reason. She was thinking snakes and alligators, for starters. Ezekiel sensed her change of mood and grabbed hold of the fence to attain a perch that permitted him a certain high stature as he spoke up. "The thing about being alive, I mean really alive, is to feel free to explore your world. Please do not misunderstand me. I am hardly suggesting that you go out and play on the freeway; however, I am suggesting that you play IN a free way! There is a distinction. Allow me to illustrate the point." With those words he climbed lower to grab hold of the webbed fence, secured a firm grasp and then began using his beak like a fine tool to peck incessantly against the old lock until its mechanism gave way. Not only was Ezekiel patient in his application, his intent was firm; and that appeared to break the lock's equal resolve to hold steady. As this singular impediment fell to earth appeasing the law of gravity, the bird looked up, proud of his achievement and boldly stated, "Done!" He checked Cassandra's more than bewildered response and continued to make his case. "It's my contention that the more you discover about the world, the more you will love and thus take care of it. Someone's got to figure that out soon, my little friend. Besides, I happen to know of a wondrous spot where a very comfortable log rests alongside a picturesque pond. I have determined that very place will serve as your impromptu schoolroom. Any questions?" He paused for a mere instant. "Any answers?" And as the child sought to follow his remarkable line of questioning, catching about fifty percent of his well-seasoned humor, she nodded in assent; but in the back of her mind, she wondered what her mother, or father for that matter, might say about Ezekiel's odd educational methods! And worse still, they had scarce begun! A mix of fear and wonder enveloped her; but she had come this far, the gateway lay open, and curiosity compelled her to walk further.

Once they crossed the gateway, it was evident that the bird spoke with no hyperbole when he described the lovely setting they soon came upon. It was perfectly picturesque. Cassandra fell in love with it at first sight. She was conscious that they would have to be considerate of the time factor, lest Grandfather return for lunch and notice the two missing. It would not be otherwise difficult to lose track of time in so compelling a setting as this! She sat down on the log as if it was placed there for that express purpose and took in the scenery, paying special attention to the way the beams of light filtered down from the sun through so many thousand leaves. The rays splintered as if heaven itself poured down casting an aura of pure magic over their little hideaway. From now on this secret place would become her official magic spot. Everyone needed, or rather deserved one, she thought to herself. Meanwhile Ezekiel climbed down and began to poke about the rich earth. Cassandra realized being in such an enchanted place was not only her treat but served him equally well, as the poor thing had been too long imprisoned in his cage. He seemed to relish walking freely on the ground, and in no time appeared to find what he was apparently scouting for. He turned to face her with a long slender stick protruding from his beak. She had the distinct feeling class was about to begin.

"Is this going to be a science class?" Cassandra asked, not so cheerily anticipating the curriculum.

Deftly placing his pointer next to his foot, Ezekiel cleared his throat and answered. "Well, I am more of the mind to expand science, which is to say, move beyond what it ordinarily observes to note a great many things usually shrouded in secrecy, some might say even mystery. Science, you see, dear girl, more often than not forgets that key ingredient known as imagination! And, as is too often the case as shown by the likes of your own illustrious Grandfather, proud researchers project their own assumptions onto their experiments; and seek to fulfill their preconceived expectations. Where is the discovery in that, I ask you?"

She hardly knew how to respond. This was all so new to her. Of course in school science was highly regarded; and she looked forward to those experiments soon to be done on frog corpses once she moved up a grade or two. That was until Gregory made her acquaintance. A playful, feisty frog, he began to do tricks to gain her attention. It seemed that Ezekiel grew a bit jealous of the new sidekick that had emerged from the pond habitat. "Alas, Gregory is at it again! Why for the likes of me, I have never met a frog with so much chutzpah. His story is a fascinating one for I am privy to it. The long and short of it is that his family migrated a very, very long way to get Gregory out of harm's way. You see the ponds of today are hardly the safe accommodating pools of yesterday. This one you gaze upon is a notable exception. The vast majority is filled with cigarette cartons, old bear cans, broken shards of glass, and other discarded remnants of so-called modern culture. Not very hospitable to the safety of those who have been long taught to make way by jumping from lily pad to lily pad. Gregory had the dubious privilege of learning a thing or two about a less orthodox way to bio-locomote across his old neighborhood pond. That was precisely why his family relocated to this one. However, that is a long story; perhaps one he will choose to elaborate on another day. It will add a good dose of humor to your journal."

"You know about my journal?"

"I couldn't help but notice the creative way you busied yourself across the past few rainy days. Frankly, I think it's an excellent hobby. And by the time summer is over, you will be grateful to have diligently kept track of the many things learned. Which reminds me: class has now officially begun! And what will we be focusing on today? Why, that's elemental, Dr. Watson. Consider that clue number one!"

Ezekiel took the pointer stick in his beak and walked about using it to draw attention to specific rocks, mounds of dirt, and other earthy objects. Dropping the poker, he spoke up, "Do you have any idea what I am doing?"

Cassandra shrugged. To compensate for feeling clueless, she added, "But I like watching you do it."

"Close but no cigar!" The parrot quipped, wondering if she would turn out to be a slower student than he anticipated. "Is it any exaggeration of the facts to suggest that you live here, which is to say on this earth?"

"Correct," she responded respectfully.

"Then the goal of my little song and dance routine is to make you earth-wise. Are you willing to advance that notion any further on your own?" Noting the young girl's discomfort, he decided to drop more clues. "There are four basic elements in this world: earth, air, fire and water. My objective here is to render you elementally savvy. And please do not despair, for there is more than method to my apparent madness. After all not everyone is elected to serve as honored guest to a queen."

"Honored guest? A queen? Me?"

"Quite right; but all things will be explained to you in due time. For now, we must learn our lessons and pass our exams." The sound of that word (exams) gave rise to fear and trepidation. Cassandra had no way of predicting, no less knowing, how severe a taskmaster this wily bird might turn out to be! For a split second she considered making a run for it and leaving him there, but what would she say to Grandfather? It was apparent that she had gotten herself into something of a tight corner. Surely it could be no worse to remain there and face the odd studies, then run away and leave Ezekiel to a fate of ill-chosen chaos. Choices! Darn! This already felt like school; but it was hardly an ordinary classroom. While she still deliberated, he began his own version of a lecture.

"What do you suppose would qualify you, a bright young person, to attain the status of the sufficiently earth wise?" Noticing that Cassandra appeared to register a complete blank, he continued. "Is not the earth the source of the grain processed into the cereal you enjoy so much? Is it not the home of the aromatic flowers, the place where animals graze, the haven from which forests bloom to share their shade, their very fruits with the likes of you? Nor have we sufficiently covered the caves where much of the ore, gemstones, diamonds form guided by the patient hand of time. Indeed it is the gold, the oil, coal and copper that make nations rich. Where is the thanks? You see the great Earth, my dear, is a living being. As such it deserves your respect. So in the interest of furthering your progress with due dedication to your gaining genuine earth wisdom, I advise a simple recipe: that you honor what you eat, conserve what you choose to use, and further demonstrate yourself to be a sound steward of earth's bountiful resources so long as you shall live. In this manner you will set an example for others, and by hopeful extension, they will grow earth wise as a healthy result. Can you imagine if this faculty became positively contagious"!

Everything he stated, rather eloquently in fact, felt true to Cassandra. Perhaps she would get the gist of what he was trying to convey. Summer school might not be as abhorrent as she had expected.

"And one can never become too air-wise, either? Would you like to hazard a guess as to what that category might consist of?" The bird pointed his question, and then his poker at the now quite intrigued young lady.

"Well, if being earth-wise means conserving what I use; is being air wise conserving my breath? Except I have to breathe air, right?"

"What else might you ascribe to the layers of atmosphere all around you? Do they not convey the sounds of every creature? Carry your satellite, Internet, radio, cell-phone and what-not signals? Air functions as a boundless railway system of sorts. It generously conducts all forms of thought, carries untold messages and communications near and far. To become air-wise, you must pay closer attention to the power of your thought; for the mind, like any vehicle, is influenced by where you park it." The very notion left Cassandra in giggles. After all, how could one park their mind? "Ah, you think that is funny, do you? But it may not be so funny to the air element that must dispose of nonsensical thoughts, angry thoughts, and worse still a great many vengeful thoughts."

"I don't have any vengeful thoughts!" Cassandra protested.

"Fine, then. But unfortunately, a great many do. Trust me, I, myself, like all winged beings am a creature of the air; and I can't even begin to tell you how polluted it has become with horrendous ruminations! Horrific protestations! This is one realm where indeed, the garbage has long built up; and it sorely needs to be taken out and away. The problem is, until people recognize the way they have filled this medium with toxic outbursts, they will not be of sufficient clarity to change it! And that is where you come in."

"Me? What do you mean?"

"The more children that become air-wise, the more the atmosphere will reciprocally improve. It has the power to clear itself, if only the right ideas become animate there. And they do, and they will through young gifted minds like yours, sending splendid cogitation, cerebration, deliberation, meditation, and alas conjecture skyward and beyond!"

For a minute there Cassandra wondered if he wasn't getting a little too carried away with his own lively diatribe. And she couldn't help noticing where the sun had climbed. If the two did not return to the house before Grandfather, how would she explain why Ezekiel was missing from his cage? At this point, she was sure they'd have to sprint back the entire way, lest Grandfather run late; but he so seldom did. He lived by his watch. It was as adhered to him as the shell to the turtle.

"Ezekiel! I think I get it. Really. But I'm afraid we may not get back in time! Were Grandfather to return before us, I'd have a lot of explaining to do.

He just might hide the key to your cage, and then where would our lessons go? Plus I wouldn't be able to meet the queen, either. Right?" Cassandra was visibly upset by this dark prospect.

"Alas! How right you are. Demonstrating yourself to be time-wise opens the door to a whole new line of study I had not quite considered! Should the tenth ray fail to mention it, I'll be sure to include it in my upgraded curriculum to be shared with my next eligible student. By all means then; let's make haste! Make haste!" And he scuttled over to the log and quickly climbed her arm to the obligatory shoulder perch. Then the two fairly skipped off together back through the now open gate. Cassandra gently placed the lock back so that it would appear to be secure. Now only the two of them would know the distinction with certainty! This slight deception served the larger pursuit of Truth, thus neither believed any real harm was being done.

In no time they found themselves back in Grandfather's sunny kitchen. Ezekiel was practically thrown into his cage so that its door could be slammed shut literally seconds before Grandfather entered. "Narrow escape," he muttered to himself, while Cassandra was left to ponder where that pesky lock had disappeared? Oops! It had fallen to the floor! No time to replace it with Grandfather heading just then into the kitchen; but fortunately he would engage his full concentration upon the fastidious task of washing his hands. While his back was turned, she gingerly replaced the lock to Ezekiel's cage. Grandfather did not hear her breathe a sigh of relief when that small but not insignificant detail was satisfied. By then Cassandra all too badly needed to wash up; so off to the bathroom she sauntered, only then realizing that she was hungry indeed!

Unbeknownst to Cassandra, the Professor had a surprise for her that afternoon. They were bound for town to do some shopping! No spaghetti sauce or pesticide show-tunes today! They'd have lunch in an open-air café adjacent to a country market that sold real organic produce. It would be there and then that Cassandra would find herself fascinated by a rich and colorful array of seeds. Grandfather was pleased to see his own flesh drawn to science when she asked politely if he would buy her several varieties, so that she could make note of which grew fastest and in what soil beds. "That's it! Experiment!" he thought to himself, aloud.

Ezekiel was also somewhat relieved to be back in his cage. He had forgotten that teaching with passion extracted a price, energetically speaking. In other words, he was grateful for a respite. He delighted himself in a nap filled with sweet dreams while the professor showed the precocious youngster the small town that had been his choice from the moment he laid eyes upon it three decades prior. Although the actual cottage purchase occurred before Ezekiel became a fixture of Erroneous' life, it was not until the professor entered into official retirement and came to live on the property year round, that he elected to have Ezekiel there as his personal companion. But Ezekiel realized a larger plan at work. Perhaps while the parrot dreamed, he was himself guided by those mysterious beings that whisper in little birds' ears the inspired doctrines and directions that separate the ordinary teachers from the memorable ones. He very much hoped to fall into the latter category. His resolve and dedication were unimpeachable, and besides, he rather liked peaches!

He must have slept deeply, for Cassandra returned with her Grandfather near sundown. She seemed excited entering the kitchen with her own prized package of what Ezekiel would later learn to be seeds consisting of varied sorts. Content that she had found the right shelf upon which to place her new treasure, she dashed off to the bathroom to wash her hands, and then returned to help Grandfather not only set the table, but get some pasta and fresh greens steaming. From time to time she winked at the bird, not wishing to give away their special relationship. Grandfather seemed to notice an unusual reticence in the bird's general demeanor.

"You haven't done anything to tease Ezekiel have you, child? He seems so out of sorts."

"No, Grandfather."

"Have you given him something to eat that doesn't agree with him?"

"No, Grandfather. I wouldn't do that."

"I wonder what the blazes it is? Probably some damned insect pest got into the kitchen and took a good size bite out of him. He's seldom this quiet."

Just to humor the old boy, Ezekiel could no longer resist (besides, he had every reason to prove his mental and physical competence, lest the professor REALLY poison him with some supposed medical concoction) and so he bellowed out the clichéd, "Polly wanna cracker? Hablar Espagnol? Polly Wanna Cracker!"

And the professor could not be more tickled pink. In fact he was absolutely delighted. His world was returned to order. So pleased was he that he'd put off his nightly researches to spend quality time with Cassandra, who was all too prepared to show off her latest sketches. Indeed, she had captured a veritable likeness of Ezekiel in her private sketchpad; and her renderings of plants were equally well executed. Turns out Grandfather was so glad to share quality time with his scion, one generation removed, that he popped up suddenly from his chair to remove a picture from its place on the living room wall. Cassandra spied the safe built right behind the artful appendage. In the blink of an eye,

Grandfather opened it and secured a small treasure. He plunked down a solid gold coin, a remnant of another time she rightly presumed.

"It is my privilege to give you this token, Granddaughter, as I am inordinately proud of you; and can already note in your keen observations, a yearning for the same kind of scientific thinking that has made me who I am!"

Cassandra picked up the shining gift, looked it over, and then gave her Grandfather a perfunctory kiss on his balding forehead. "Thanks, Gramps. I never held a real gold coin before!"

"Well, that's just the tip of the iceberg to the treasure trove waiting upon this very estate." With those words he gave the young girl a wink; and then went into his study, lit a lamp, and sat down with his favorite book. Cassandra followed him quietly; then chose the smallest seat in the room, an old rocking chair that her Grandmother must have once sat in while knitting. It now found a new behind to rock; not that Cassandra was particularly interested in sewing of any sort. She too would read, or write in her journal, or color, or cultivate her artistic inclinations by fashioning a special still life. Later she could render its likeness in her journal for memory's sake. Who knows, perhaps one day it would be her own grandchild who sat in that very rocker, flipping the yellowing pages of her journal, and thereby traveling back through time to see and experience what she had in these sweet memorable moments.

Ezekiel went back to sleep. He just didn't fancy himself an artiste!

RETURN TO THE MAGIC SPOT

Bright sunshine fairly danced around the room providing an invitation to a new day's potential adventures. Ezekiel caught the mood. No sooner did Cassandra enter the kitchen, did he begin his strange whistling sound.

"Whatever is that?" She questioned.

"Just getting a beat on your level of alertness, dear girl. As you no doubt have noticed, it's an extraordinary day. In fact, a perfect day to resume our lessons, once you have had your breakfast and changed your clothing into a more suitable attire. Shorts will just not do when you have a population of hungry mosquitoes lurking around the pond!"

On warm, sunny days it was practically a reflex for Cassandra to choose loose fitting shorts and a colorful t-shirt to wear. But of course, the parrot was right. When it came to mosquitoes, she placed confidence in Grandfather's work. Who wouldn't want to rid the world of those atrocious little beasts? The patient bird watched and waited as Cassandra savored every crunch; today she added a banana to her cereal bowl. After clearing the table, rinsing her dish, and dutifully changing her clothing; she climbed to retrieve the key that would lead the two to new horizons. Besides, by now she was not only accustomed to the allure of new discovery; she rather liked the sensation of a bird on her arm. She doubted if any pirate could wear one more respectfully!

This time as the two made way toward the property's rear hidden gateway, they watched for strategically placed spider webs, armies of marching fire ants, and the occasional beetle moving his highway load. There were a fair number of striking butterflies that seemed to flit about as if flirtation was all they lived for. She loved the careful arrangement of color on their glittering wings. The walk went quickly since she now knew where they were headed. Actually she found herself eager to return to the magic spot. It definitely held allure. The pond was as lovely as a gem inlaid into emerald greenery. This time the sun's rays shimmered down from a changed angle. Clouds filtered them while they gently crossed the heavens above. She developed a fondness for the spot; and even welcomed the no doubt unconventional lessons the seriously studious bird would soon initiate. School in the wilds was more interesting than she had expected; but before she could resume her comfy place on the fallen log, Ezekiel said, "I have a surprise for you."

"I can meet the queen?" Her retort shall we say jumped the gun.

"Not yet my dear; you have scarce finished your classes! Now, come along," he said, leading her toward a dense thicket of underbrush. He bent over to get hold of a bunch of bright purple berries as Cassandra's fingers reached up to scoop away most of the bounty. "Have a taste of this! A treat from the earth in appreciation of your attentiveness during yesterday's elemental class." She all but glowed as she chewed the delectable fruit so unexpectedly come upon. Ezekiel deftly drew several berries, one after another, for his own pleasure. "Well, that should do it, a bona fide morning snack. Now, let's get back to our studies, shall we?"

With those words, the two trailed back over to the log, and Ezekiel climbed down to his favored spot to secure his poker. A teacher ought never be without a poker, thought he. "Were I to ask you to review what you hypothetically mastered yesterday, what would you say?"

"That the world out here is represented by four key elements."

"Excellent!" The bird responded, pleased that the youngster absorbed his words while making them understandably her own. "And did I mention in yesterday's haste to get back before Grandfather noted our absence, that when one becomes earth-wise they recognize that rocks are to the earth, what bones are to our own bodies? Or that in becoming air-wise, we acknowledge a notable exchange with our good neighbors, the trees. Do you know what I am specifically referring to, Cassandra?"

"Plants create photosynthesis and convert carbon dioxide into oxygen, so we can breathe."

"Why that's first class, child! Thus you might rightly conclude that the great forests function as the lungs to our planet. Alas, we must take care of the trees for we are partners in this enterprise called life, are we not? And that takes us to the next element in succession: water. Do you dare to anticipate my next question?" The bird certainly meant to keep Cassandra on her toes by continually testing the quickness of her mind.

"How does one learn to become water-wise?" She showed clear moxie, even imitating his personal style of elocution!

"Right! For eleven points," he added with unabashed humor. "And what do you suspect that would entail?"

"To learn to go swimming and not be afraid of the water?" She answered with a fair measure of logic.

"That's a start, a fit and fitting answer; but I'd like to pursue the matter, shall we say, from a more elemental standpoint. If the rocks are earth's bones, and the trees earth's lungs; what then would you surmise the waters, streams, rivers, and ocean beds to be?"

"The blood!" Cassandra noted, with a strain of genetic scientific savvy inherited from a Grandfather not too many footsteps, and yet worlds, away.

"Indeed, you are correct! Now as to the function of water, elementally speaking, it facilitates in you the capacity to feel. Have you ever heard it said that poets and mystics search out the still waters? It is there that their sentiments tap into the well of deep inspiration."

"Hmm." She answered, rather solemnly.

"I see. It could be said that water is essentially complex. After all, it readily changes states: from liquid to boiling steam, from rushing downhill to freezing into thick blocks of ice. In its magnetic powerful way it invites us to feel the state of our world together. We are born from a watery medium, in your case the embryonic sac, in mine the albumen of the egg. When you feel what another feels, you experience a powerful invisible bridge known as empathy. And as each being grows in his capacity to feel such connections the result is that no one need feel separate, distinct, or entirely alone. For once this knowing is established, one recognizes that they are truly related to everything else. So it's a great thing to become water-wise, you see; for it prompts you to take greater care of other creatures, as well as yourself."

Cassandra appeared to struggle in taking in the bigness of the ideas he presented to her. Ezekiel, however, knew he could count upon her memory; for ideas, planted there like seeds would grow when the time was ripe to do so. Besides he had no time other than the present to plant those seedlings! Necessity prompted him (as it does all great teachers) to consider altering his methods. He was determined to get through to her! And so for comic relief the bold bird grabbed a light stone in each claw. Then he leaned back, nearly falling over, while managing to clang them together like gongs. Cassandra nearly fell over with laughter, herself.

"What was that? A lesson in balance-wise. Not!" She offered comically.

"Yes. Well, it got your attention, didn't it? We are going to have something of a change of pace here. I sense that your mind has reached its full-zone. Rather than have new ideas spill over and get wasted, we shall explore a different approach. Perhaps you will like it. I am going to ask you to empty your mind, that is to say, still your thoughts."

"You mean try not to think of ANY thing?" She quipped back, already sensing the difficulty this might entail. How could one not think, when there was so much to think about? It was a very, very odd request to be sure; she thought silently to herself.

"Yes. Give that a try. Let's see if you can clear your mind; turn it into a crystal clear fishbowl. Except there will be NO fish swimming about, is that understood?"

In visualizing this scene within the confines of her mind, all kinds of rebel thoughts burst through. Cassandra imagined they just might be the very fish she was trying so desperately to keep outside of the imaginary aquarium! She began to fidget. Then she fidgeted some more. It was impossible for the bird not to recognize her discomfort.

"Hmm. We must provide this enterprise with a decidedly more dedicated application. For alas, until you master the full elemental curricula I am not authorized to extend Queen Buzz-bee's summer birthday bash invitation to you."

"Okay. I'll try harder." She promised; and she meant it.

"Consider that your every thought is a firefly. They certainly will blink off and on with a seeming will of their own; however you can at will turn all their lights out. Now just allow yourself to be with the darkness for several moments. Try that."

Surprisingly, when Ezekiel provided her with a new picture, she found less resistance. Soon she was able to remain within a blank state, a quiet state while moments passed by. Ezekiel led her to a place that felt like it existed outside of time. The bird left Cassandra in that still zone before once again, not unlike a puppeteer's toy, suddenly seizing the impulse to gong the two stones together. The cacophonous clank returned her to ordinary attention. She looked like someone unexpectedly awakened from a full night's sleep, not to mention dreams. He gave her a moment to reorient her perceptions.

"Now this type of tuning as I will henceforth refer to it, serves as an important precursor to your meeting the twelve rays, honored guests at Queen Buzz-bee's bash. Rest assured none will be more honored there than you, young lady! And I am pleased to say I am duly noting progress in your tutelage. Good job! Besides, that also means that I am doing a good job, since it has fallen to me to prepare you." Having said this, he used one of his wings to pat himself robustly on his back. The odd gesture left Cassandra in absolute stitches.

"I never had to prepare for a party before where I closed my eyes to bring my mind to a complete stop. Of course I've closed my eyes to play 'pin the tail on the donkey.' But that was ages ago."

"Well, there are a great many things you have probably never been asked, or asked to do for that matter. Let's try this one. Do you happen to speak French?"

"No."

"How about Italian?"

"Nope."

"Would you by any chance happen to know what the whale's chilling plaintive sea song seeks to express?"

"Nope. I never even heard it!"

"Aha! Precisely! Nor have you heard the ants, quite sociable ones at that like Tidy-up and Nutra as they discuss the newsworthy items they come upon amid their daily routines. So you see, you have missed quite a lot."

She giggled ostensibly at the very thought of such nonsense.

"You find this funny? Let me remind you that up until rather recently you were perfectly prepared to limit my language paradigm to something as ludicrous as 'Polly wanna cracker.' In spite of that, I have made every effort to disabuse you of such stereotypic notions. Now, if you expect to be a charming party guest, you will have to do better than this! For it would do you no good to enter a world, a lively one to say the least, where you could neither speak, nor understand the languages being spoken. Alas! I did say languages; for as many as there are creatures upon this earth, are there languages being spoken. Just because you don't speak Swahili, hardly means no dialog in that lingo is underway. Keep that in mind, dear girl. Today's exercise in tuning deep into the quiet mind is a key step to opening your perceptual portals so that you may find yourself quite fluent in dialects you have scarcely heard of!" Pumped up from his own impassioned diatribe the bird marched back to his favorite berry bush to devour yet a few more tasty treats; for he had all but burned out his available energy supply. As a matter of fact, the sun was already creeping to its noon summit, and they'd best soon be on their way. Hardly were the elemental lessons fulfilled to perfection; but he knew there was no point rushing what took others whole lifetimes to grasp. Still, Ezekiel faced something of a personal dilemma in that the queen's summer bash was just scant days ahead! For him education was more than a job; it was a bona fide calling. He held fast to his faith that Cassandra would get the hang of it and prove an admirable guest debutante for Queen Buzz-bee's ball.

While the bird inwardly reflected on his student's progress, Cassandra hoped that she had not deflated his noble expectations. These were new, strange, and difficult concepts to digest. She sincerely wished to learn quickly. After all, the Queen's bash was not something she intended to miss. It was not like she'd gain access to such a unique invitation once she returned home! Her mind grew pensive as the parrot climbed up to her shoulder. Both were silent as they hiked back to the Professor's kitchen. She worried if Grandfather ever altered his strict regimen to return home early? Hopefully, if his routine ever took such a twist, she prayed it would either occur on a rainy day; or after her lessons were completed, and the much awaited Queen Buzz-bee's ball behind her!

Nothing eventful interrupted the flow of the day's later activities; although evening brought the light of the nearly full moon directly into the professor's study. It would prove a challenge to fall asleep as voices from the pond (a hundred thousand crickets and their hungry frog captors) triggered by the luminous moon's call echoed throughout Grandfather's cottage. Seized in rapture the motley crew would rhapsody their off-key love songs the whole night. And Ezekiel had much on his mind as well. The almost full moon was the ticket to the summer's best bash; and no one, not even a reluctant human student, would keep the royal Queen Buzz-bee waiting. The task facing him was enormous. It consumed him. Could this promising student quickly catch up on her studies, lest they both otherwise find themselves out of the anticipated social loop? Somehow he managed to sleep in spite of his concerns; and so did Cassandra.

As fate would have it, the wind currents from the Gulf brought yet another sudden rainstorm straight toward the professor's sanctuary. Lightning was brisk and rain came down with unremitting gusto. For Ezekiel the clock was ticking. Mandatory elemental classes were already running behind; and as a result of the inclement weather they'd lost yet another precious day of instruction. Meanwhile, the professor seemed to enjoy the diversion. He broke with custom. Instead of donning his ridiculously out of fashion raincoat and rushing through the downpour to his laboratory, he elected to watch old *Sherlock Holmes* movies in black and white on his aging VCR. Cassandra seemed to enjoy them, too. They chose to take a voluntary intermission so they could make popcorn in the microwave; fortunately Cassandra was careful to sneak a few crunchy kernels to Ezekiel. She knew he was bored; so it was only fitting that she show him a token of her appreciation. Given Grandfather's scrutinizing eyes, that small gesture was the best she could deliver under the circumstances.

Ezekiel couldn't remember when he fell asleep; but he didn't miss much. The professor must have played that same video a hundred times. To the wise and seasoned parrot, *Sherlock Holmes* was old news.

FINAL PREPARATIONS

It was a relief when the sun returned the following morning; and a second relief that Cassandra had at last arrived at the breakfast table. Ezekiel was an early riser; however, Cassandra was not. In any case, he stood by as she satisfied her morning routine, and when all the details were attended to, she knew what was expected of her. Doing her best to keep pace with the bird's thus far unspoken expectations, she believed she had met every item. Without any audible direction, Cassandra collected the bird and together the two left the cottage. They made quite a pair almost resembling Siamese twins of albeit slightly separate species. Perhaps in the quietude she would practice the tuning of her mind to his. A pall of seriousness fell over them both as they realized there was more than fun and games awaiting them.

It turned out to be a good thing that Cassandra was not one to rise at dawn, for the log had needed the sun's fresh morning rays to dry off from recent rains. A wet sit upon would hardly prove comfortable; and what would Grandfather say if he spotted her wearing wet clothing? As Ezekiel climbed down and assumed his favorite spot upon the ground, she took a moment to compose herself. Like a dedicated classroom student, she would review her notes thus far; even if these existed only in her mind. Since she had already learned the basics of becoming earth-wise, air-wise, and water-wise; the only thing remaining was fire; and she knew how dangerous it could be.

Ezekiel's words took her by surprise. "All right then. As you may have surmised, the final element we wish to discuss today is fire; and it presents us with an ageless mystery. For indeed while science can explain the way thermal forces operate, no one can truly explain from where the flame derives. In fact, your ancestors looked upon fire as a veritable gift from the gods. Today human beings have indoor heating; but can you imagine the power of the flame to protect and ensure early human life in the wilds when winter dropped its fierce blankets of snow? One must behold fire with a certain awe; for it reflects a great and primal mystery. And in that mystery, you may come to recognize the limits of your own perception. This understanding should humble you. For in the face of utter vastness, you note with certainty that all that may BE known indeed is not yet known. Thus no one need put on any airs. To become fire-wise is to recognize that something mysterious guides you. It exists beyond you; and yet it can also direct you from a place deep within, for in many respects fire is the quintessence of light. Mystery, you see! Sometimes it will incline you to be cautious, this voice that protects. Other times, it may sweep you up upon the very wings of passion. Fire is the spark that makes you the unique being that you are. It speaks the breath of the great spirit that has created all of this!" His wings then opened to symbolically embrace the full expanse of time and space. "Be advised that fire can both consume a forest with an incomprehensibly brilliant burn; or rejuvenate it like the phoenix arising from its own ashes. Do you understand?"

"I believe so," she responded with marked maturity. Her growing elemental savvy began to show.

"Then there you have it! The elements in all their fundamental wisdom portrayed. That ought to serve as basic curricula for every student, if you ask me. And I suppose you have, or why would I be out here?" Before Cassandra had a chance to laugh aloud, he continued, "Now we must progress to our previous exercises in the quiet tuning of the mind. Can you summon the image of the empty fishbowl on your own, or that of fireflies pulsing? I can otherwise devise an alternative guided course to lead you into the interior quiet zone." However before the bird had a chance to finish diagramming his lesson plan, Cassandra had already anticipated his aim. She began to still her thoughts, and was able to enter the empty place more readily than he would have otherwise predicted. He found himself pleasantly surprised and rather amazed. This exercise after all was a significant precursor to that final and most crucial of tests. Only if she passed it was he prepared to present Cassandra as a worthy guest to the royal queen at her much anticipated birthday bash.

He began to pace back and forth like an expectant father in a hospital delivery room. When that did nothing to alleviate his nervousness, he started counting numbers in his head. Of course he certainly had to provide Cassandra with ample time to prepare herself for the final challenge. "Where is the professor's watch when it's needed most?" Ezekiel mumbled to himself. Perhaps he could number each time he circled the log on his wobbly legs; and then formulate from this quotient a sense of minutes passed. No point leaving Cassandra indefinitely under the sway of the mind's hidden undertow.

To humor himself he suddenly realized the exercise was rather like baking a cake. It could neither stay in the oven too long a time, nor too little, were it to fulfill its destiny as a cake! In parallel fashion Cassandra would have to develop the capacity to sustain a sufficient state of receptivity wherein advanced language skills could develop. If he broke her concentration before she had mastered that keen ability, what value would his carefully executed lesson plans amount to? There was much hope attached to the progress of her inner tunings. With a firm sense of determination now acquired, Ezekiel believed the cake was ready to emerge from the oven!

"Cassandra? Cassandra? Are you with us, dear girl?"

Once again she appeared groggy as she adjusted her eyes to the immediate sights set before them. It was as if she had been transported to a distant place, and now had to reacquaint herself with the present surroundings. And what did she see but a simply adorable turtle slowly making his way from the pond toward the very log she sat upon!

"A volunteer! Excellent!" Ezekiel proclaimed. Cassandra hadn't the faintest idea what he meant; but she trusted he would waste no time in explaining. "If you put your now tuned mind to the task, I believe you can listen and hear what this turtle has to say, or perhaps ask."

Her previous habit was to challenge the logic of such a notion; but something had inwardly shifted for she decided to test her new ability while also satisfying Ezekiel's odd request. She looked at the turtle intently, and quickly realized it would be best to get closer to him. After all, this was apt to prove something of an impromptu interview! As she lifted herself from the log, Ezekiel said nothing; nor did he try to stop her. Walking with slow, deliberate moves Cassandra drew nearer to the turtle. At first it reflexively drew its little green and yellow head into its shell; but then he popped it out and she swore she could hear him say, "I just wish you'd tell all your kin folk to slow down. Slow down! Is that such a lot to ask?" And then the agitated turtle got right back on his way.

Stunned less by the turtle's words, than by the fact that she'd heard them; she awkwardly backed up towards Ezekiel. It's not like she expected the turtle to ask her to pick him a daisy, but the experience was a bit disconcerting. She hoped for words of counsel or confirmation from Ezekiel. He, however, was caught up in a review of the results to his own experiment, and fairly brimmed over with satisfaction.

"What did the turtle say to you?" He asked cheerily.

"The turtle told me to tell my kin folk to slow down. He asked if slowing down was too much to ask. Did he have to be so rude?"

"Excellent. And as for the rudeness, if you ask me turtles get high marks in my book. They are very intelligent creatures, you know, and patient, too. They're just not given to crossing highways at the speed of your present day cars and trucks. Nature didn't make them that way. So they're having a hard time of it, what your kind calls progress, that is. Still, they are quite marvelous in their own right, don't you think?"

"Well, yes." She conceded giving the matter deeper thought. "I always wanted a turtle for a pet; but my Dad didn't think it was such a good idea. He said they belong outside in their own ponds."

"I was not speaking of a turtle as a house pet. That is quite another matter. Which brings me to the question: do you know yet who I am?" He asked pointedly.

"Ezekiel!" She answered, not expecting any trick questions.

"Perhaps I am your familiar," he countered.

"My familiar? You mean my family?" She ventured her best guess back at him.

"A familiar is to the lay person an apparent pet; but to the wise, a special companion, one gifted with shall we say powers. Of late it has become crystal clear to me that I have been standing by at your Grandfather's estate until fate saw fit to cross your pathway with mine."

That was a lot for Cassandra to absorb. Understandably it left her with no immediate comment. However, the bird continued his enterprise of planting new seed thoughts in her now quiet mind. In due time they would produce their own harvest. Changing the subject, she interjected, "Well? What about the test I need to pass to be ready to meet a real queen?"

"Done!" The bird joyously responded. Cassandra looked at him as if waiting for some riddle or disclaimer. When the bird did not provide either she put her mental tuning fork to work and began to read his thoughts. He appeared to court the opportunity for her to do just that!

"Is it that in talking with the turtle I proved I could hear one of those other languages you were talking about?"

"Yes. That's exactly it. Now don't presume you can speak all of them at once, no less discern their differences. There are many, and they vary in subtlety and composition. This type of skill comes about gradually. However, it's clear that you are getting the gist of it. Besides, the main thing was to remove your resistance so that listening to other beings was made possible. Once the mind can be taught to maintain quiet, a great many things deemed impossible indeed prove quite the reverse. These uncharted fields of the mind can often be explained by and through intuition, which bypasses the need for direct translation. The twelve rays will provide you with your next communication challenge; but it should pose no barrier given what you've already proven yourself capable of demonstrating. Trust yourself, my dear; and allow instinct to guide the rest! And if instinct serves me well, I'd say it's about time we got going. Let's not tempt the fates. We must not give Grandfather the slightest reason to suspect us; after all we are about to slip off for a truly grand escape, I mean occasion. The invitation should reach us shortly if all the key pieces fall into place, as I suspect they shall!"

With those words, the two began a quite enthusiastic trek back to Grandfather's cottage. They arrived with time to spare. As a result Cassandra was able to gently return Ezekiel to his cage, secure the lock, wash up; and appear as a perfect homebound angel before Grandfather arrived, no less to suspect the slightest glitch in apparent conditions.

She wasn't the only one sitting proud at the lunch table. If the professor had feathers, they'd have been puffed to full extension around his small stout frame. He was absolutely pumped up, and it wasn't long before Cassandra learned the reason why. He did not reveal the news directly. It was only when he busied himself with several animated telephone calls before he had scarce finished lunch that she picked up on what was taking place. Seems he had come upon some unexpected breakthrough in his research. Instead of returning promptly to his laboratory after lunch, as was his usual custom, he sat Cassandra down to make something of an announcement.

"Granddaughter dear, a very important development has emerged in my research; and I must apologize to you. However it's absolutely urgent that I share my findings with my two most trusted colleagues. I have invited the much-esteemed professor Felix Quackenbush, and his loyal assistant Millicent Killjoy for dinner tomorrow evening. Promptly thereafter we will convene in my laboratory. Cassandra, I have every confidence that you can find productive ways to busy yourself about the cottage in my absence. I fear our trio will be working long hours into the night as this research is absolutely vital! There is nothing like peer review in my line of work, Granddaughter. If by some fluke of procedure, I should have missed or discounted a critical detail, I must leave it to my associates to pick up the slack. Will these plans be all right with you dear? Just this once? I fully expect to be home every night hereafter; so please do not feel the least bit slighted. Again, let me assure you that this work is very important! Forgive me this exception, would you Granddaughter?"

"Of course, Grandfather. Everything will be just fine. Ezekiel keeps me company."

Looking over at the bird with a dubious expression Grandfather continued, "Yes. I've noticed. You two appear to have bonded rather intently. I suppose that's what happens when there's no one your age available to play with. But out here in the woods, I'm afraid there are no close neighbors. I purchased this property for solitude and quiet research, not to socialize with young neighbors. However, once my present line of research is concluded, you will have my undivided attention! Perhaps we can find some games to play, though I must confess, I am rather rusty when it comes to recreation. I make a better scientist; and generally prefer to direct the utility of my mind toward the solving of problems, the conducting of research, collecting data, and the like. You could say that testing the limits of my own intelligence is my favorite game. Therefore toys, amusements and related pursuits have never been my forte."

The professor grew flustered as if all at once he recognized the hundred details he'd need to attend to before his friends' anticipated arrival. He left the study in a whirlwind leaving Cassandra just a few prized private minutes with Ezekiel. If the parrot had hands to clap, that's exactly what he would have done at that very moment. However as fate would have it he was limited to expressing himself with words, as Mercurial creatures tend to do. "Well this must be kismet! Circumstances have indeed conspired. For I dare say a substantial amount of behind the scenes cosmic choreography is expeditiously underway!"

"Ezekiel, I don't mean to appear rude; but can you translate that into English, please?"

"What I wish to draw your attention to my dear is the ripeness of the moment. Fortuitous, indeed! Your Grandfather will be sworn to his researches and busy at the lab the very night not only of the summer moon full enough to guide our safe passage, but this in synchronicity with the very special and much awaited evening planned for Queen Buzz-bee's ball! One could not ask for more perfect timing! Honestly, I feel as excited as a schoolgirl. Wait a minute, YOU should be saying that!"

"I am excited! I just don't know what it is exactly that I am to be excited about. I'll have to find that out when I get there!"

"An evening that will be long remembered; why I dare say you'll be telling YOUR grandchildren about it one day! It's practically history in the making! And besides, there is something to be said for the art of anticipation!"

Cassandra gave that concept some thought; but no sooner did the bird seize the moment's opportunity to lay out the upcoming plans, did the professor return. He had found linens and placed them in a pile on the kitchen table. "Cassandra would you mind helping me fold these napkins?" As Cassandra took the first one in her hands, she realized that it was too early to set the table for the next night's dinner guests. After all, they'd scarce finished lunch; and then there would be dinner, followed by the morning's breakfast. It made her wonder if her grandfather kept track of time at all? What would he do without his trusty watch? He came dangerously close to fitting the cartoon stereotype of the absentminded professor. Erroneous practically blew in and out of the room on some invisible wind that kept reversing its direction. It seemed he was nervously given to inventing the oddest of tasks to accomplish. Cassandra did her best to please him, and was honestly delighted when nightfall came. Indeed, she was tired. Besides, if there really was a grand ball, and if she was to be the honored guest of a queen; she'd store up sleep while she could. That way, she'd be at her best and brightest to make a royal impression on the dignitary. Quite possibly her dreams led her through ancient castle hallways to elegant closets where she was privileged to try on ballroom dresses of the finest silks. Just what should one wear to a great ball? A restless part of her mind sought to satisfy this probing question while her body lay in repose till morning arrived courtesy of Apollo's chariot.

INVITATION TO A QUEEN'S BALL

Cassandra entered the kitchen as if it was just another day. Her demeanor appeared nonchalant as she breathed in the peace and serenity of country living. The mood would not last long. She went about her tasks and sat down to her favorite crunchy granola. Naturally she presumed that Grandfather was doing what he always did, which is to say busying himself with work at his laboratory; but scarcely before she finished her breakfast did he appear in the room. Fortunately, Ezekiel had no plan for a clandestine outing on his morning agenda. It was a very good thing that her required classes were completed to his satisfaction. Before she rose from the table to wash her dish, Grandfather laid a list out beside her. On it he delineated all sorts of small jobs he hoped to satisfy before the evening's company was due to arrive. Apparently Cassandra would have cause to earn her keep! But no worries, mate, she was capable of adapting herself to the demands of the moment. What with the anticipation of the Queen's ball occupying her thoughts, time would pass very quickly. The first matter of business on Grandfather's list was to cut up fresh vegetables for a dip. His guests were instructed, as it turned out, to bring items for a potluck dinner. Grandfather's contribution would include hot chili, a favorite recipe he guarded along with his "delicious/delocious" pesticide secret sauce, and numerous healthy vegetables to snack upon. Cassandra found the cutting board, and chose a sharp knife, though not the sharpest. She rinsed the cucumbers, carrots, and tomatoes and began cutting narrow strips of each. Why not bring her artistic skills to the task she reasoned? And so she laid the cut slices in a design that soon rendered the whole platter a grand flower of sorts. It was of course imperative that she maintain a fixed focus on the cutting, lest she accidentally slice into a finger. However, something kept catching her attention out of the corner of her right eye. After nearly cutting herself more than once, she slammed down the knife to obtain a closer look at whatever was scurrying about. Sure enough, she caught sight not of one roach, but an entire roach family each taking turns sneaking across the kitchen floor. They ingeniously took cover under the cabinets having long practice in making their way to chosen destinations and safe hiding places. Darned if the largest was not carrying something bright and shiny!

Ezekiel watched the drama unfold, and since Grandfather was temporarily out of earshot, he advised: "Well, this is the perfect time to put your tuning to work. What do you think?"

The parrot was right; however, she didn't really want to get too close to the roaches. On the other hand she was awfully curious about what they were up to. Edging as near as her sensibilities would allow, she cleared her mind and made an earnest attempt to listen to what the roach family might have to say. Unbelievably, they turned out to be enormously chatty! First they politely introduced themselves as the Concha family. Then they went on to say that they recognized they were not necessarily welcome in Erroneous' home; but that they came from a long line that preferred the better built houses, having witnessed their share of floods, hurricanes, and so forth. Next they railed on about their considerable excitement as they, too, were invited to Queen Buzz-bee's ball. As a matter of fact they made it a point to sort through their considerable collection of heirlooms, things passed down across a lineage that had spanned many generations to arrive at a suitable gift for the queen. In fact, so impressed were they with Cassandra's courtesy and attentiveness that they offered to privilege her with a private showing. Prior to this offer she had no idea of the variety of riches that existed behind Grandfather's walls! To suspend her doubts the Conchas reminded her that human families across the ages had oftentimes noticed things missing. Generally they attributed such losses to 'the borrowers,' thought to be the cause behind these varied and common displacements of articles. The Conchas wished then and there to make it perfectly clear that they were not borrowers at all; that they preferred to think of themselves as investors. After all, they had taken note of the fact that ordinary objects accrued considerable value, oftentimes enormous value, over time. The comfortable roach family was prepared to go on with their lengthy explanation of inherited wealth; but Cassandra had heard enough. She backed away from the little family just in time for Grandfather's footsteps could already be heard heading from the study toward the kitchen. "Hurry up!" She yelled. And while her words were intended to protect the little roach family she had just been formerly introduced to, Grandfather naturally presumed they were directed at him.

"I'm moving as fast as I can. What is it? You didn't cut yourself on those cucumber slices did you?"

"No, Grandfather."

"Then what's all the hurry about?"

Knowing she'd need to come up with a logical alibi, she thought quickly. "I can't reach the garlic. I thought you'd want me to cut up some cloves for your chili."

Grandfather looked as if someone had caught him with his hand in the cookie jar. "Oh, you noticed my garlic?" He queried. "No one knows for certain what I put in my secret chili sauce!"

"Grandfather, that's not much of a secret. It's common sense. Everyone uses garlic in their chili sauce."

Erroneous reached up into the floating net he had suspended from the ceiling. It held produce situated there to hasten the ripening process. He took a large garlic floret from the net and placed it on the table. "So this is what you were in such a hurry over? Honestly child, you'd think a vampire was on the loose!"

Cassandra laughed, but it was to cover up her clandestine encounter with the roaches. She really didn't find Grandfather's joke too funny. From that point on she did her best to fulfill the chores he requested; and once they were all completed, the afternoon just seemed to drag. It was a difficult thing to wait for a party! So she spent time writing in her journal, sketching, and reading; but all the while she missed sharing outdoor adventures with Ezekiel. The whole house began to smell from Grandfather's chili sauce which proved a genuinely inviting aroma. She'd never really seen her Grandfather entertain guests before, and wondered what he'd be like in the company of people his own age? That would be an experiment worth observing, she thought. Once the professor was satisfied that his own obligatory tasks were done, he sat down in his study and smoked a pipe she thought just existed for show on his mantelpiece.

"I never saw you smoke that pipe before, Grandfather?"

"Tonight is a special occasion. It relaxes me," he said, holding up his pipe. "If my research is half as successful as I hope it to be, many things will change in the world, and in this house!" He proclaimed. Then looking the youngster over he made a rather novel request. "Granddaughter, I'd much appreciate it if you combed your hair and put on one of your frocks. Let's make a good impression on my guests tonight, shall we?"

Although she was not really in the mood to wear a dress, it was not a request that asked much of her. If so simple a thing could give Grandfather pleasure she'd accept the temporary discomfort. Besides, Grandfather had mentioned that right after dinner the trio would convene in his lab. She could off the dress and quickly assemble a more fitting attire for hiking through the outdoor vegetation once the time was ripe to do so. The secret plan she harbored made her feel rather like a criminal masterminding a means to a covert escape. As was true of all such enterprises, she would need to maintain ordinary appearances until it was time to enact the hidden agenda. So she gently got up from the rocking chair and entered her room to rummage through the chest that held her things. She had two dresses packed there just in case. This was an appropriate occasion to make use of one. And since she was going to wear a dress, why not dab on a bit of perfume, and embrace the whole feminine experience? Indeed, that is what she did. Repeating the grooming rituals of lost ages imprinted upon the memory banks of the "gentler sex," she succumbed to combing and styling her hair, washing her face and then applying creamy lotions; and ultimately becoming transfixed with the transformed image reflected back at her from the bathroom mirror. It was the sudden commotion that snapped her attention back to present reality. Indeed, Grandfather's guests had noisily arrived.

When Cassandra entered the hallway to greet his colleagues, she could not have expected to see a more incongruous trio. Professor Felix Quackenbush towered over Grandfather like a tall, reed-thin pine tree. Millicent Killjoy had evidently not applied her notable lab skills to anything so pertinent as the intended uses of hair dye. Indeed, her coiffure simulated an autumn sunset. It was so red it could stop traffic. The guests made way with food platters as Grandfather directed them into the kitchen. The chili smelled enticing so no one wasted any time before sampling it. The vegetable hors d'oeuvres proved just as delightful. Each guest seemed to indelicately reach over the other to obtain the foods now assembled on the kitchen table. In the frenzy to secure favored items, Cassandra spied Millicent inadvertently knock against Ezekiel's cage, not only destabilizing it; but nearly turning the whole thing over with its innocent bystander still inside! Fortunately, Grandfather gave it a steadying hand just in the knick of time. Cassandra stood back and observed the chaos wondering if she was hungry enough to enter and thus endure the foray. Millicent managed to surface for air between hefty bites of varied food items to say, "Oh, Cassandra. Lovely to meet you. You look so nice tonight." (Cassandra was tempted to reply: "Tonight? Why you've never seen me before to determine any difference!") Instead she smiled back politely. Felix took his plate and backed away from the narrow kitchen confines, and offered, "Cassandra, there's plenty of room. Come. Make yourself a plate. Everything's absolutely delectable. You really must join us!"

With the near catastrophe to Ezekiel's cage averted, everyone took a seat which made second helpings all the easier to obtain. The trio went on and on about this experiment, and that study; what this professor said and how that authority countered it. She had heard quite enough of scientific gibberish for one night; and just wished they'd leave and go to the lab. Wasn't that the plan? Ezekiel must have felt exactly the same way. Surely the wise bird would have a strategy under his wing to get things moving. The last thing Cassandra wanted to do was miss the ball! And then the breakthrough happened. Ezekiel in his wisdom engineered the perfect cure, lest it was payback for the lively party of three nearly crashing his cage! He all at once let out a string of dirty words that would have made a seasoned sailor blush. This ingenious, unexpected tactic had the effect of a fire drill. In no time the space was cleared out!

The Professor was too shocked to speak; while Millicent, profoundly offended, lifted out of her chair leaving the following impassioned words in her wake: "My word! Heavens! Who taught him such things"! Eying the two scientists her gaze suggested deep misgivings about the sorts of male colleagues she had devoted her time and considerable efforts towards assisting.

"Perhaps we had best retire to the lab to take stock of the more pertinent developments that summoned our meeting here this evening," Erroneous offered calmly to defuse the embarrassing mood of the moment.

Returning her gaze to the now half amused child whose sense of hilarity was only partially hidden, Millicent uttered with a hint of unmistakable maternal instinct, "Are you sure it's safe to leave Cassandra all alone in the house?"

The professor, still struggling to regain his composure and sense of authority after the parrot's outburst assured his guests. "Cassandra is hardly alone. She's got Ezekiel." When no one seemed especially charmed or remotely comforted by this assertion, he went on to say, "Besides, I've observed hers is a sedentary nature. She'll be quite content to remain at home where she can safely work on her gifted drawings, add entries to her journal, and so forth. Besides, if she needs us, she knows where to find us. She may simply knock on the laboratory door. Isn't that right, child?"

Cassandra nodded; and wishing to speed them off, not to mention bid them a prompt adieu, she added, "And don't worry about the dishes. I'll get the kitchen all spruced up. You can go now. Go ahead. I know you can barely wait to compare your research notes."

Cassandra heard Millicent echo, "What a polite and charming child," as the door slammed and the three at last left for the lab. They didn't hear the word "Freedom!" that Cassandra muffled under her breath while filling the kitchen sink with soapy water. Then with masterful efficiency she quickly cleared the plates and dropped them into the suds. Without so much as a pause, she spun around, found and deftly applied the plastic wrap to cover the leftovers, and quickly deposited them into the fridge. "I'll be right back, Zeke!" She added with a hint of comic relief, as she zoomed into her room, effortlessly tore off her dress, slid on her thickest pants, heftiest socks, tackiest sneakers, and longest sweatshirt. She was ready! "Queen Buzz-bee's ball, ready or not, here we come!"

It would have no doubt attracted the finest detective eye had he spied the way the pair popped their heads out the front cottage door in unison to check that the coast was clear. No flashlights for them, the full moon would illumine their pathway. And no sooner had they left for the backyard gate, did a cloud of fireflies find them. The troupe acted as a congenial entourage present to guide the duo in their safe passage toward the evening's festivities. It was not entirely dark out yet; but indeed the sun had set. Even so, the last brush strokes of a rainbow painted the sky directly ahead of them. It must have rained miles away, yet the beams still shone brilliantly. Ezekiel gazed at the amazing sky and said, "What a night to meet the twelve rays. Why it's as if the very heavens have opened to offer us an omen of agreement. There's nothing quite like a rainbow, is there? Look at the way its colors come to life!"

Cassandra was too filled with eager expectations to lose any momentum by stopping to answer questions. She just wanted to get there! Unbeknownst to her, events were already getting underway quite close to her magic spot, seat of the recent elemental classes. As the sun set the full moon rose. How could she adequately describe the intense feelings being drawn up inside of her? It was as if they poured from a secret pool. All at once her senses were seized by an unmistakable connection to every living being. The entire ambiance down to its minutest nuances pulsated with an electric mix of light and sound. Each and every element helped to infuse the atmosphere. It was overwhelming; and yet she felt so much a part of it all. There was not a single thought of fear. The evening reached out to take her into its embrace, and strangely she felt herself a welcome part of festivities without having ever met any of the expected guests! Odd indeed. And just as she sensed, things were about to get a whole lot stranger!

MEETING THE TWELVE RAYS

Whatever spell the enchanted spot cast over Cassandra suddenly was broken when Ezekiel let out the whoop to surpass all others! It was louder than any whistle she'd ever heard, and did the trick of gripping everyone's attention. His voice assumed a more commanding tone than she would have thought possible for a bird. And these were the admonishing words he uttered:

> "Let it be known that this circle is now officially consecrated; and that there will be neither interloper nor predator permitted to enter to take advantage of any of our guests." Ezekiel looked around in search of any flutters of dissent. Then he continued. "And if any should have a problem with this singularly clear and incontestable protocol, they will have ME to contend with. May I also remind any potential offenders within earshot that I come from the old country where breaches and transgressions are not kindly tolerated."

The mood grew momentarily dim; but then suddenly the stately bird made use of the timing device of an experienced Hollywood master of ceremonies. He let out a second more enthusiastic whoop; to which he added, "Start mixing, all of you! The Queen's birthday bash is about to begin; and I'm deliriously happy to see so many of you here for this much anticipated occasion. And now I have the pleasure of introducing my young protégé, Cassandra. Having been trained exclusively by yours truly in the ancient art of tuning, I believe you will find her to be a charming conversationalist. So please introduce yourselves; and by all means enjoy yourselves while our talented performers prepare to get the big show underway!"

As Cassandra recovered her hearing from its proximity to the shockwaves emitted by Ezekiel's whoops, she wished to walk around and introduce herself to the guests. Although in her mind's eye she had not pictured a party primarily attended by insects, she had to admit the atmosphere was electric, its magnetism undeniably compelling. Also she was interested in learning more about the tiny performers who were just then intently focusing on backstage last minute preparations. She hadn't the foggiest notion that she was already in the exclusive company of the much-touted twelve rays. Meanwhile as Ezekiel observed his young student, he came to the conclusion that it would serve no valid purpose to allow his presence to overshadow the occasion. It was clearly time for Cassandra to learn on her own. To too closely monitor her meetings might limit the unique discoveries the varied encounters promised to deliver. He therefore made an unexpected proposition to the already bedazzled young girl.

"Dear girl, seeing how Grandfather saw fit to clip my wings, my customary perch is beyond, shall we say, my grasp. Can you give me a lift?" He indicated that he wished to be assisted in reaching a tree branch just over Cassandra's head. She obliged him accordingly. The shrewd parrot recognized the benefit of overseeing the party's unusual events from a sturdy, well-placed vantage point. His chosen post would allot him a guard's scope of the range of festivities only beginning to get underway. In this way, he would ensure that no stranger interrupt the unusual gathering. Indeed, he was fully prepared to make good on his foreboding words of warning.

Cassandra gave him a long backward glance before succumbing to curiosity. Then she began her own independent exploration of the grounds carefully noting the odd variety of creatures milling about. Although on a radically miniaturized scale, the scene resembled a circus with varied performers inside their little tents preparing for their nervously awaited stage calls. It was not every day that a human child was invited to share such a unique world. Reciprocally the vast majority of local guests took a concerted interest in her. Even though she had received Ezekiel's highest recommendation and personal endorsement, she felt a lot like Gulliver being scrutinized by the tiny people of Lilliput. The only way to enjoy the festivities or otherwise converse with fellow partygoers was to put into practice what she had learned. Quickly she concentrated on tuning her mind to the myriad conversations occurring at shall we say less dense decibel levels. To do this she ever so conscientiously took in several rhythmically timed deep breaths while focusing intently. In a very real sense her brain was being trained the way an athlete gears his muscles.

Only in this case mental chambers were being modified to accommodate an elevator of sorts directed between previously unexplored "floors" of cognitive operation. Once having gotten the gist of this skill it was not difficult to listen in on the conversations already abounding among the little beings. As was often the case when food was being prepared, eaten, or delivered, the ants tended to be the first respondents to arrive on the scene. Indeed Cassandra smelled food preparations underway; but before she had a chance to follow the scent to wherever it might lead, she found herself drawn into a conversation that just happened to feature her as its primary topic!

"She doesn't appear to me to be a Too-Muchner," said a well-spoken, confident black ant.

"But it's too soon to take in the comforting notion that she might turn out to be a rare Caretaker," another equally articulate ant responded.

"Excuse me," Cassandra butted in, "But are you talking about me?"

"Indeed we are," the two responded in a small chorus. "And what of it?" They further incited.

"Well, I have never been called a Too-Muchner before. I don't even know what that is; and as for being Caretaker, what exactly is meant by that?"

"For a minute I thought she was going to criticize our penchant for utilizing labels. How would she know that specific criterion is vital to us in our work," the ant explained.

"No one works harder than we do," the other ant defended. "Who proves a more committed custodian of the earth than the ant?"

A third ant overheard the conversation and dutifully approached to build upon the consensus, "Indeed, our kind constitutes the first conservationists, ecologists, herbalists, and ever-ready clean-up crews. Isn't that right, Tidy-up?"

Cassandra recalled having crossed paths with Tidy-up several weeks earlier. My goodness, that ant got around! (She thought to herself.)

"And honestly we don't begrudge the Too-Muchners; for after all, they leave an awful lot of food behind for us!" Added Nutra. "Still, we're rather wary of all the dyes, additives, preservatives, herbicides and heaven knows how many other chemicals embedded into ordinary crumbs nowadays! It's just inordinately difficult to alter the gatherer behavior that for millennia has served the sixth ray well. As we all know habits are so very difficult to break!"

"It's all very interesting what you have to say about food crumbs and the like, but I'd really like to know more about those Too-Muchners you mentioned," Cassandra politely cut in. She was not particularly schooled in the appropriate etiquette for speaking with ants, after all.

"Ah yes. The Too-Muchners, an unfortunate class to be sure; why they're easy enough to identify. You know the ones; they spend all their time getting stuff, taking care of their great many things, and then holding onto them to the point some can barely navigate within their own homes, not to mention their over-sized bodies!" Tidy-up explained appearing impatient with the sorts.

"But they are by no means the worst of the bunch. Why the Speednaughters in their rush to get wherever it is that they are headed, notice absolutely nothing along the way. As a result a good many ants, not to mention larger living creatures, get squashed before their time. I ask you, is that fair?" The third ant, whose name she never picked up said irately.

"I don't think I'm a Too-Muchner or a Speednaughter!" Cassandra clamored in her own defense.

"Well, those are hardly the only groups humans occupy," Nutra added.

"You mean you have categories for all people?" Cassandra asked incredulously.

"Well, you certainly have categories for us! This specie, that genus, this reference, that categorization. Don't you think we have a right to do likewise?"

"I'm sorry, "Cassandra interrupted. "I didn't get your name?"

"It's Pedia, short for encyclopedia. My friends say I'm given to extrapolating great quantities of information in the shortest time-spans." The ant stated with a measure of evident pride.

"Well, can you tell me about the others so I might recognize my category?" Cassandra's tone was curiously inquisitive as she posed the question. (She imagined any thinking child confronted with this intriguing data would certainly want to know where they stood when the subject was them self!)

"Okay. There are The Programmers. They're the ones who think everything and everyone, down to the weather, is supposed to act a certain way. They're fixated on the false notion that one size suits all. Hardly true. And you'd think they'd learn from experience, modify their views when exposed to the contrary; but nothing could be farther from their truth. They just continue as if life never threw them a glitch; then it's back to their programmed drawing board a/k/a agenda all over again."

"Wow!" Cassandra responded. I hope I'm never like that. I wonder if Grandfather counts in that league?"

No one answered the question, rather Pedia continued with the larger explanation underway. "We must mention The Squanderos. Shameless. They take so much, waste the vast majority of what they take, which is to say consume; and the really sad thing is they appreciate so little."

"Senseless dissipation," I'm afraid," Nutra added. But as these words were exchanged, a virtual army of exceedingly frightening fire ants began to march right towards their little gathering!

Cassandra reflexively pulled back, when thankfully she heard the big bully ant up front, no doubt the troop's leader yell, "Okay, men. Hold your fire." To her surprise, she also made out the muffled response of one of many soldier ants as he said under his breath, "Hold my fire? All my life I've been trained to let it rip. I haven't a clue how to actually hold my fire."

Surprisingly Cassandra observed as the fire ant troop leader approached a shy little black ant who had long, flirtatious eyelashes. She's wasn't sure if it was polite to listen in, but she'd never really observed the courtship rituals of any ants before. Besides the romance bristling between the two was about as palpable as a flame. She couldn't take her attention off them.

"What's your name?" The bully ant asked the shy black ant that chemistry had unmistakably drawn him toward.

"Sister Tee," she answered shyly.

"Pretty little thing like you; do you already have a date for the queen's ball?" He asked.

"Not yet," she answered with a sparkling dose of healthy self-esteem.

"How would you like to accompany me? As you can see, I manage a rather large battalion of soldier ants. They're all in top shape, thanks to my daily disciplined sunrise drills and related exercises."

"Perhaps I would respect your work more if all that manpower was used to build something constructive, like say a hospital for young, wounded ants. Seems to me it's currently serving a rather destructive ends."

Cassandra had never heard a tiny creature speak with so much power. Naturally she wondered how the tough bully ant would respond.

"Our skills have come about by necessity, the mother of all inventions. We got tired of the kingdoms of all the small creatures being summarily crushed, poisoned, shoved aside, and thrown off their native lands to make way for every new human development. We decided to fight back!"

"I understand entirely," she said tenderly to defuse his defensiveness. "However, if you only equip the strong to survive, what kind of planet will be left for your kind? I implore you to consider using your collective power for a more noble purpose. I understand that you feel powerless against the forces . . ." But before she could complete the thought, the irate fire ant roared back, "Powerless? Look at these muscles!" Indeed he flexed his tiny form to prove himself mighty.

"I am not questioning your strength," she countered patiently. "I am merely suggesting that power serve a more creative and constructive ends. There is a different, quite remarkable power to be found in building alternatives to the old ways; and you would be surprised to find out how good you felt about yourself in the pursuit of such endeavors, especially when what you do is done for others. Others who quite possibly do not carry the strength that you do to accomplish these productive things for themselves." With those inspired words she batted her long languid eyelashes, and he seemed to all but fall under her spell.

"Well, no one can argue that we come from different worlds; but I appreciate your point of view, and the eloquent way that you convey it. I am prepared to keep an open mind and give your advice due consideration." Then acceding to the lovely black ant's charms, for chemistry is known to work wonders, the fiery bully placed his arm in hers and the two would have walked off together, had not one of his troops let on.

"Hey! What about us?" A daring singular voice echoed from the ranks of fire ants still assembled at attention.

Throwing them a backward glance, for after all, it was a party night and they all awaited his orders to join in the festivities, the leader responded, "All right men. No pillaging or plundering. You're on leave; but remember to behave like trained soldiers at all times! We'll assemble tomorrow at dawn, as usual. Be ready."

With those words the fire ants set out in pursuit of whatever adventures the night might bring.

No longer feeling any imminent sense of threat, Cassandra resumed the unfinished conversation she had been sharing with the black ants. She was intrigued with their observations, and wished to complete her understanding of all possible categories that people fell into. However, the tempo of the crowd was beginning to rise to a fever pitch, and the ants had no intention of missing out on the action. They were in the mood to circulate and indulge their social natures before everyone's attention would be directed to the stage where a talent show in honor of the queen would soon boast the best of well-rehearsed performances. Sensing their desire to move on, she tried to finesse them into sharing a bit more data.

"Did you leave out any categories?" Cassandra asked.

"We really ought be getting on our way," Pedia noted; but then realizing that the information meant a lot to the young girl she offered, "Well then, just follow along with us, why don't you. We can discuss the matter as we cover ground."

Sure enough once they began walking Tidy-Up responded to Cassandra's honest question. "Have we mentioned The Blenders? They're the types that don't like to rock the boat. They prefer to fit in with whatever people surround them. As a result they can be rather bland. For you see they seldom voice independent opinions. Instead they prefer not to make any waves. We believe such types to be insecure; or otherwise hardly self-realized."

"The Examiners interest us most. That's because they look so deeply into everything and anything. They take expeditions, shoot video footage, research the wonders of the world and often generously share much with others who don't have the stamina or temperament to go off after such exhilarating answers with the passionate gusto they do. We prefer to connect with those sorts."

"And The Examiners get along splendidly with The Pollinators." The trio of ants stopped to catch their breath, while Cassandra likewise measured her footsteps into tiny baby steps so they all could walk together.

"Why do The Examiners get along with The Pollinators?" Cassandra found herself asking with due regard.

"Mainly because The Pollinators set about to meet precisely the people who can show or tell them something new and unique about life or the world. The Pollinators thrive on sharing their views with people of different cultures, countries, communities . . . you name it!"

"I think I could be a Pollinator or an Examiner," Cassandra conjectured aloud.

"Alas, but there are also The Semblancers. Be very careful of those, my dear," Nutra offered as the ants suddenly picked up tempo. They walked the full circle and observed a good many backstage performers. In a very real way the lively show was already underway.

"What can you tell me about The Semblancers?" She asked while walking ever so slowly and carefully, lest she run over a creature attempting to speed by across her path.

"They place inordinate value on things that are fake and persons that are phony. We're not sure they can even tell the real from the artificial, quite frankly," Tidy-up related.

"And we find The Reverse-The-Clockers a bit tragic, I dare say," Pedia added. "Poor things lost in some legendary time when life was all but perfect. They don't dare live in the present. Current challenges prove too formidable for their minds to bear."

"Is that it then?" Cassandra asked, now a bit anxious herself to mix with other creatures before the show began. She made it a point to commit all those details the ants related to memory.

"The Toasteetadors burn up in anger over anything, and I mean the slightest most nonsensical trifles," Nutra imparted. "Thankfully you're not one of those!"

"Can I be a wizard or mystic or wonderer? Not a wanderer, the kind of person who walks without direction; but a wonderer, someone whose mind travels everywhere instead." She inquired resolutely, knowing full well that if anyone knew the answer to that question it would probably be those ants.

"Well. There are always new categories to be developed, no less discovered," the trio of ants assured. Cassandra took that as an affirmative vote; and with their nod of approval she bid them adieu. Then she carefully picked up the tempo of her own footsteps. But no sooner had she done so, darned if she didn't spy her pink ribbon stuck within the glowing strands of a strategically placed spider web. This time she was well prepared to carefully avoid it, having learned from a previous mistake how not to invite the silky tendrils to fold like glue over her face. The spider stood by and observed Cassandra who was, however, prepared to reach in to collect her ribbon.

"Not so fast," the spider quipped. "I must advise you that whatever enters the web is most assuredly destined to remain there." There was a chilling aspect to her utterance.

Cassandra looked at the spider, a rather large one at that; and was not sure she was prepared to challenge its assertion. Just in time a firefly came buzzing by, blinking on and off with electric gusto. The encounter elicited a sudden feeling of déjà vu in Cassandra who remembered her "catch" earlier that summer.

"Haven't we met before?" She blurted out.

"That wasn't me. It was a distant cousin; but I heard that you set her free; and I thank you for that; since light like ours was never meant to be bottled up in a jar!"

"How did you find out about that?" Cassandra went on to inquire.

"Well, my dear, news travels fast at the speed of light!" Before taking her leave she further advised, "And I would not reach into her web, if I were you. Take a look at what's in there. Word has it the remains of a very unfortunate ex has become a lasting souvenir."

Beguila looked back at the youngster once the firefly buzzed off. Cassandra sought to return her gaze; however it seemed that the creature had turned upside down to reveal an altogether different side of her persona. It was hard to be sure it was the same spider?

"People tend not to like us," the spider stated regretfully, "but that's chiefly because they seldom see our good side." With those words she flipped a second time.

"You could show me your good side by returning my ribbon." Cassandra quipped. Then the spider flipped over yet again. It was beginning to make Cassandra feel dizzy!

"My good side? Did I say that? I must have contradicted myself!"

"Why don't you make up your mind?" Cassandra asked impatiently.

"Make up my mind? Why heavens. Which one? I pride myself on having two, for after all there are a great many to choose from! However, if you're having trouble keeping track of my prerogatives, I will generously extend to you a fuller education. For you see I am scheduled to artistically portray twin perspectives during my critically acclaimed kabuki theatre performance which will be featured on stage in no time! Stay tuned!"

So much for reclaiming her ribbon. As Cassandra diligently continued her explorations with countless creatures scurrying about, she noticed some mightily focused bugs busy at work fabricating an apparent miniature stage platform. She heard one yell out, "Hey, Guido, where do you want the steps to go?" She watched as a large termite boasting a gleaming gold chain around his neck made way to check on the structure being built before her charmed eyes. He looked straight up at Cassandra and said, "A bug's got to be determined. My family's been in the construction business for eons. I've got a cousin in South Florida who makes a killing in this line of work." Then pointing at a mound not far off in the distance he added, "You see that mound over there? You know what I could rent that for? It's got everything. A prime location! Great for a big family; well, maybe not YOUR big family." He seemed to suddenly realize his sales pitch was not quite right for Cassandra. "Mounds are something I happen to know quite well; and I mean the highs and lows of the whole construction enterprise. We go way back. Who do you think taught the Egyptians how to build?"

"You mean the pyramids?" Cassandra asked incredulously.

"That's right. My family knows how to construct the stuff that stands up to the tests of time." Then as if his nose serendipitously guided him toward some invisible nether world, he asked, "You smell that? That's the genius of my wife Fifi Alfredo. She's catering this whole affair. What that termite can do with wood is in a league all its own; why your world-class European chefs could not touch what my Fifi does with wood. And she's no stranger to conservation, either. No, sir! That termite does wonders with what she's got to work with." Guido was tempted to break out into his best operatic voice to express his love for the delicate flavors that filled his world; but he wisely decided to restrain himself, as the singing waiters would soon enough have their voices heard passing through the crowd with platters of the finest beech, elm, pine and fir. And besides, he would offer a solo for the queen in due time. Instead he decided to show his hospitality in yet another distinctive way.

"Not everyone knows this about me," he offered in quiet tones, "but I am what you might call a Renaissance bug. I live to eat, and I eat to live; but I also happen to harbor an equal appreciation of beauty. Now if you follow me just over this way to your right, behind that mound, I'd like to show you my personal rock garden. It's where I sit when I need to collect my thoughts. I relish this peaceful spot," he added. "It reflects the Zen part of my personality." She had no idea what he was talking about, but indeed her eyes soon grew enchanted with the lovely little well-apportioned domain he introduced her to. It never dawned on her that a termite might have a sense of aesthetics guiding the mounds he was given to build. Plants were carefully situated with a clear sensitivity toward design in evidence. Fairly certain that he had gained her confidence, he decided to take advantage of the occasion by sharing key lessons he had acquired in his satisfying life as a termite. After all, Buzz-bee's ball was a prized occasion, and he wasn't altogether sure he'd ever meet up with the young girl again. "I want to tell you something, and advice don't come cheap. You know what's important in life?" It sounded like a rhetorical question since he didn't give Cassandra much time to answer. "Foundation! Laying down roots! Making things secure for your loved ones. It's as true for me as it is for you. And I didn't catch your name either?" He all but interrupted himself.

"My name is Cassandra; pleased to meet you."

"Likewise. My name is Guido, affectionately known to my peers as the second ray. And another thing, you'll do well in this world in any business; if you do what comes naturally to you."

"Yes. That sounds like good advice. Now may I ask you a question? If you're the second ray; who is the first?"

"Had any encounters with fire ants lately?" He asked her.

"Yes. Just a little while ago," she responded.

"Well, they're the first ray, and I'm the second. Beguila, the spider, she's the third, and so on. Chances are you'll get to meet the whole circle tonight. That's what this shindig is all about. The queen is a great benefactor; and she loves theatrical events. Besides, everyone knows she throws the best party of the season. Wouldn't miss it for anything, which reminds me, I gotta get going. Fifi might need some assistance in the kitchen. There's a whole lotta mouths to feed here tonight! Now if I could only track down Woody, Jr." He spoke while almost ingesting the very atmosphere in one intense breath. "Ah, the senses, what they do to me! Do you smell that? It's the breath of trees on the breeze. Ah, the bewitching scent of these. I tell you it makes me hungry. 'Cause if the flowers smell good, imagine the flavor of the wood! Can I help it if I was born with a ravenous appetite? I just love to eat. As a matter of fact, you will have the culinary treat of your life, tonight. So enjoy yourself. It's nice to have met you."

With those words the most determined bug she'd ever met indeed got quickly on his way leaving Cassandra to wonder when the show would actually begin. She noticed that crickets were busily assembling pine needles into a cozy looking pile; but she did not yet realize they were preparing her seat of honor next to the queen who was always prepared to arrive in fashionably late style. No formal performances could scarce begin until her highness gave a sign of readiness. It was then that Cassandra's eyes fell upon a large, strange looking grasshopper who appeared to have Rastafarian knots of hair about his head. He was so intent on what he was doing, he scarce noticed her stare. The grasshopper, who she would come to learn was known as E.Z. Hopper, expertly turned over a mushroom to inspect it, before beginning to pound it rhythmically to invoke the sounds of a conga. He then did likewise to two or three other mushrooms of varied sizes. Her ear (or was it the toning exercises?) was sufficiently sensitized to recognize the differing sounds being emitted. The expressive grasshopper then placed a tiny seed gourd next to the mushrooms; and it wasn't long before she realized he had assembled a set of drums of the oddest sort which he played with diligent dedication. He was obviously well practiced in the art of using nature's objects to evoke different rhythms and vibrations. She observed the wondrous creature apparently lost in the music of his own making. Yet just then he seemed to sense the intrusion of someone's gaze, someone who was not familiar to his world or ways.

"Hey man, I was into a groove. Traveling the rhythms; language of symbols and ancient utterances," he said; although his words might as well have been Chinese to Cassandra. Taking note of the young girl's perplexed countenance he put out his long lean hand so as to cordially venture a handshake. "Name's E.Z. Hopper. I'm the musical director for the queen's outrageous summer birthday bash. Pleased to meet you. And you are?"

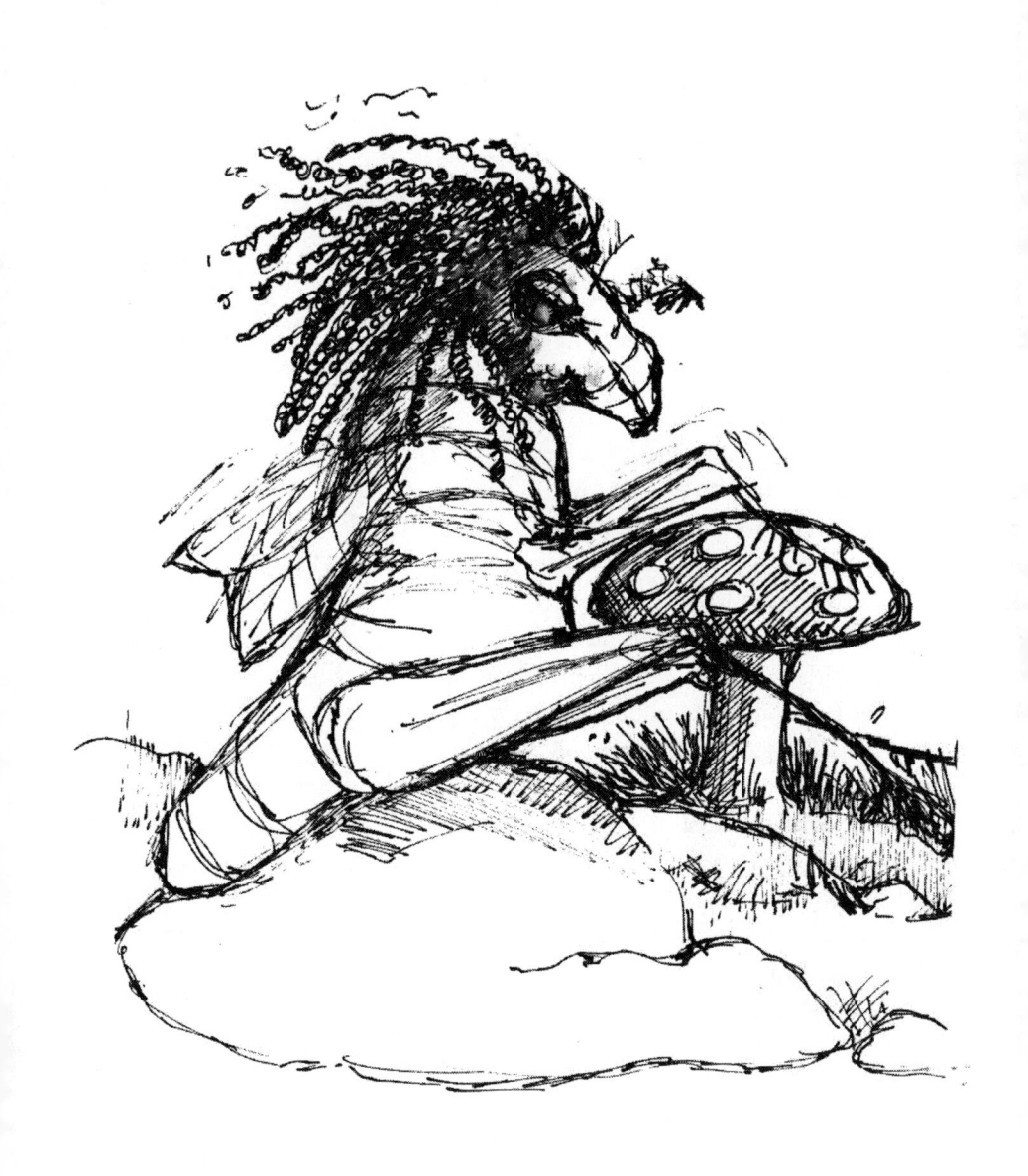

Still stunned, Cassandra reached down to offer her much larger hand to his: and she quickly recovered her capacity to respond. "My name is Cassandra."

"Oh, yeah. Little bird; or maybe it was a big bird, come to think of it, told me you're the honored guest tonight, huh? Probably never been to a party like this one. Can you dig?"

"Dig?" She answered with more of a question, for it seemed he was referring to her recent introduction to Guido, who indeed was more adept at digging.

"Just musical jargon," he elaborated. "I mean do you like to dance, move to the beat?" He asked. Cassandra had never really thought about it; although at that very moment, as if on cue, two fireflies buzzed by. She couldn't help notice how their pulses seemed to strangely align. She heard one say to the other, "You turn me on!" Then the other responded, "Yeah. We better watch our charges or we just might black out the nearest city!" Not entirely sure what they meant since all the dialects being spoken were so new to her, she felt somewhat off balance with all that her little brain was struggling to take in. She wished the show would start. Where was Queen Buzz-bee? With no royal monarch in sight, her attention returned to E.Z. Hopper who began to fashion some blades of grass into apparent tiny wind instruments. He was very good at what he did.

"It's all about sound," he half-mumbled to himself. "Sonance: great quality there. It's the sensation caused by vibrating wave motion perceived by the organs of hearing. Take a look at this thing's acoustics," he said, indicating the underside of the mushroom directly in front of him. "It's built like an accordion, perfect for reflecting the entire decibel range."

Cassandra's expression spoke volumes. It was clear to E.Z. Hopper that she just wasn't getting it. He'd have to prove himself a formidable educator to get his point across.

"Decibel, you dig? It's a unit for measuring the volume of sound, equal to the logarithm of the ratio of the intensity of the sound to the intensity of an arbitrarily chosen standard. Got it?" He fairly glowed with pride for what he took to be a most excellent explanation.

Cassandra had an entirely different view, however; and wondered if that smarty-pants was just showing off. She decided to ask him something she had always wanted to know now that she managed to secure his complete attention.

"You must be very intelligent to be able to make all these instruments; and you seem to know so much about sound. So how come I always see so many grasshoppers crushed in the middle of the road? Don't you all know it's dangerous to cross busy streets?"

His eyes were almost human in the way they gazed up at her as he prepared to answer, "Sweetheart . . . that's the risk we take for discovery. Go ahead and call us reckless. There's just something so compelling about that search for the next horizon. It's what drives us to cross the great divide in eager pursuit of the need to know more of just about everything. The ninth ray was built to travel far and wide. It's a passion planted deep inside. That's pretty much how I see it." Charmed by his own explanation, he spontaneously and not the least bit self-consciously added, "Hey. That ought to be in a song! Gotta remember that for a future show tune." As soon as he uttered those words of self-praise a graceful entourage began. Two lines of adoring ladybugs formed and began their march towards the pine needle mound. Up until that moment Cassandra hadn't noticed the fragrant lily just then electing to send its spray of night perfume into the abounding air. Now she understood! What could possibly serve as a more fitting best seat in the house for a queen bee than a splendid evening flower blooming gloriously in her apparent honor? But Cassandra had scarce laid eyes on the actual dignitary. Still, the ladybugs instructed her to take her seat like the others. It was evident that the Queen was about to make her royal entrance.

Cassandra sat down on the little hill of pine needles and found it to be wonderfully cozy and equally comfortable. Several ladybugs took positions near her. One said, "There's no mistaking the queen's arrival. There's such an obvious buzz about her!" Meanwhile another ladybug with mild disrespect offered; "But honestly, her children are such royal pests!"

Wasting no time in picking up the proper cue, E.Z. Hopper began a drum roll that reverberated from his private collection of mushrooms. Countless crickets lent their unique blend of percussion to give the sound a fuller body. Then lady Beguila, the spider, deftly plucked the chords in her web, while a tall praying mantis, not yet introduced to Cassandra, probed strings set against a large seed gourd. This ad hoc jazz trio provided just the right mood music to accompany the queen's much anticipated arrival. Maybe it was the way music stirred souls, but all at once Cassandra felt genuinely excited and rather proud to be a queen's honored guest! Her toning and elemental studies had served her well. This was the prize those efforts had won; and much more was soon to unfold!

SHOWTIME!

A flurry of fireflies shone their pulsing lights to make way for the Queen's arrival. Cassandra could see plainly that the royal one had style; and it was not solely due to the fascinating honeycomb she wore gracefully atop her head like a regal crown. She moved with confidence; even though it was the countless ladybugs in waiting that made sure the royal bee arrived safely seated upon an elegant lily leaf. There she would look out over the evening's offerings with a marvelous view of the stage below, itself just completed by the industrious termite builder team.

Cassandra had never sat next to a bee before, no less a Queen bee; and she wondered if her manners would prove sufficient to satisfy the occasion. The Queen only nodded at her, subtly acknowledging her presence. Evidently this was her party and she would play the role of master of ceremonies to the hilt! E.Z. Hopper took the stage as countless fireflies blinked at such a fast pace it seemed that Hollywood's own spotlights were shining.

The jazz-cool grasshopper bellowed, "And now for the greatest little show on earth!" Having said that he appeared to wait for a further signal from the Queen. Then he expertly changed the rhythm to an upbeat crowd pleaser to move the audience to a heightened expression of enthusiasm. When a fabulous mood filled the air, the Queen began to speak from her perch; and while equipped with no microphone, nature endowed her with something in the order of strong lungs because she certainly could bellow out her words. They practically hung in the air, still resonating moments after they were spoken.

"I am absolutely delighted to see so many of you gathered here for my summer birthday bash; and what a line-up of entertainers we have for you tonight! Let's start with a round of applause for my musical director, E.Z. Hopper."

The crowd let out all kinds of hoots, hollers, clucks, and related sounds of apparent favor.

"As you know, later on we'll be passing out those coveted 'Golden Honey Awards' so many of you look forward to each year at this time. The fruit of our hive, tonight's awards are sculpted from the finest honey in a time-honored recipe that draws upon liquid light from the sun." The Queen continued, "And may I also introduce, for those of you who have not yet had the pleasure of her company, our first human guest, who has been prepped for the occasion by none other than the illustrious professor-bird, Ezekiel. Please welcome Ms. Cassandra."

As the crowd clapped and cheered the parrot (close enough to the undertakings to conscientiously acknowledge being acknowledged) took a modest bow from the tree perch he maintained. Indeed he proved steadfast in his resolve to keep watch over the festivities occurring below. Although Cassandra was a bit puzzled as to why the Queen referred to him as 'professor,' she certainly would not be so rude as to interrupt the dignitary in her commencement address. Still it seemed as if the whole crowd was staring at Cassandra; and she wondered if she was expected to also take a bow? Instead she raised her right hand and waved at all the guests, hoping the action would not produce sufficient air current to knock the royal bee off her delicate lily perch. Such a diversion would cut considerably into her guest of honor status; and no doubt close the door to any future invitations.

"Our first performance this evening is being presented by a lovely member of the third ray, Beguila, who will share a Kabuki theatre enactment with us. Let's give her a preparatory round of applause, shall we?"

The Queen's wishes were ultimately commands; so the crowd sympathetically obliged. The fireflies must have done a bit of rehearsing for this number. Their pulsing lights illumined the elaborate strands that brought to life the spider's skilled weave-works. Beguila as it turned out had painted one half of her face pure white, and the other black. As E.Z. Hopper drummed eerie rhythms on his organic drum set, Cassandra wondered if it was Guido blowing into a reed that issued plaintive tones not unlike those from a flute! The graceful spider used half visible silken strands to freeze her movements in a variety of difficult postures, almost like a gymnast rendering a routine on the uneven parallel bars. The crowd was mesmerized by first seeing the spider's bright happy face, then suddenly its stark reversal. The changing views the spider projected reminded Cassandra of the masks that depict comedy and tragedy upon the human theatrical stage.

As the performance continued, Cassandra could smell something raw, rich and fertile. Sure enough a crew of termites, adorned in white aprons, made way through the crowd carrying trays with no doubt woody delights atop them. For the first time the Queen spoke to Cassandra, "I prefer to be waited on royally. If you ask me, service is not what it used to be." Then checking Cassandra's expression as if she could read straight into her heart, the bee posed the question, "Do you have the faintest idea what Beguila is trying to convey in this . . . act of hers?"

As if on cue, one ladybug recalling that the queen had trouble with foreign translations, offered her help. "Your excellency, what Beguila artistically seeks to express is the contrast between positive and negative approaches. Her movements project a palpable sense of paradox. She relates the poignant fact that life's quality is essentially a matter of perspective."

"All that, huh?" The queen responded with a note of sarcasm. She seemed genuinely pleased when the performance was finished. A responsive round of applause followed. Quickly a discrete ladybug approached the queen to whisper in her ear. Immediately thereafter the Queen rose and likewise lifted her voice to announce to the crowd, "And our beloved Guido will now share with us an operetta that he composed. Let's give him our utmost attentiveness."

Again lights illumined the stage. Guido gleamed under their pulsating glare. Before beginning his performance he graciously dedicated the song first to Queen Buzz-bee, and then to his loyal wife and companion, Fifi Alfredo. And even though Guido was hardly large by any standard, he seemed to take on enormous proportions once he opened to the power of his song which was rendered in basso profundo.

"Recall the shimmering stillness
Where all gifts reside?
It's that which gave Mozart his music,
And Renoir his eyes.
Out of the mystery that shapes all time
Our senses are brought to life, sublime.
So I sing praises to maple, birch, and pine
Inspired flavors, each equally Divine.
Have you ever sampled oak, elm, or fir?
If you had, you'd naturally concur.
So eat up friends, the hors d'oeuvres are hot;
And you could not be sharing company in a better spot!"

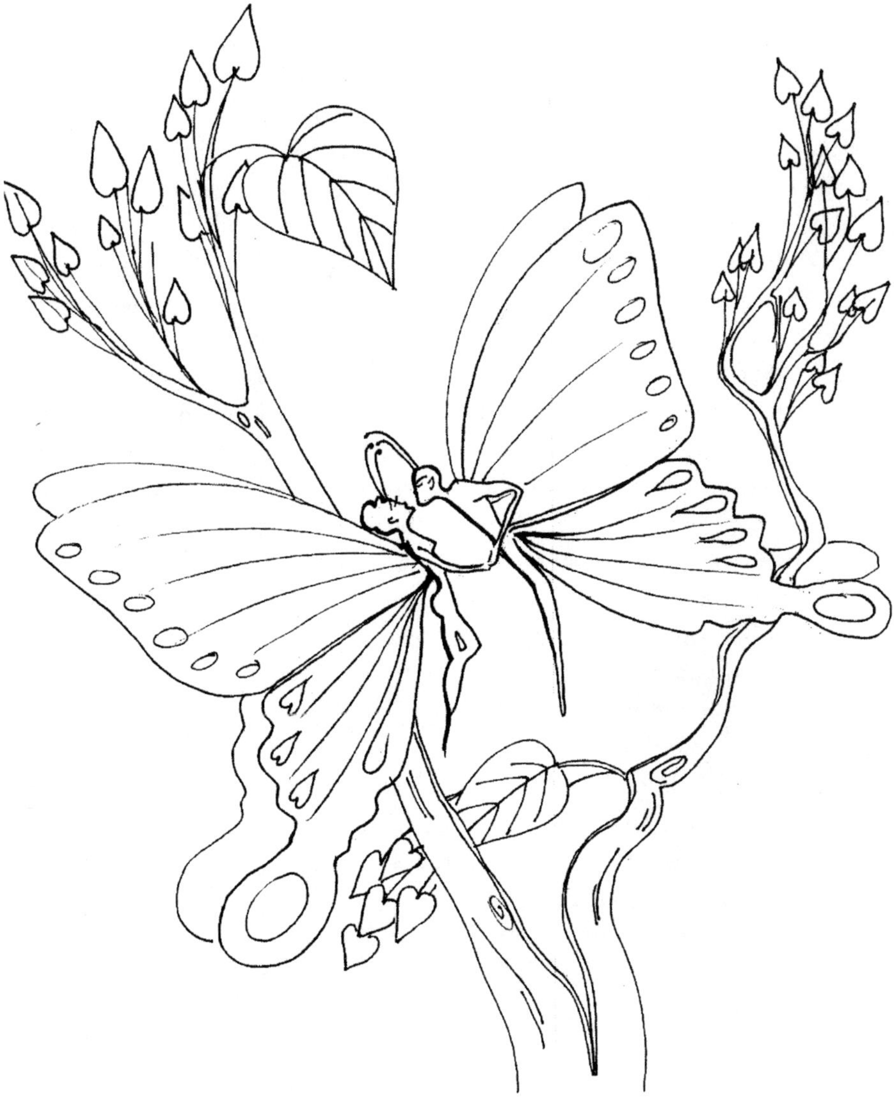

The Queen seemed especially charmed by his performance. And let out a loud buzz of unabashed approval. The sound initially caused Cassandra a bit of a fright. She knew better than to cross the path of a buzzing bee, Queen or otherwise. It simply was not prudent. Then right on schedule another ladybug arrived, no doubt to remind the Queen of the next act that required announcing. Cassandra was pleased with the orderly way the insects came together to share in such a notable occasion.

"May I now present the Alluras, the famed dancing duo from our circle of ever so talented rays! Let's give them a big hand," she robustly encouraged.

The crowd responded with fiery gusto. Cassandra edged forward to look closer at the absolutely dazzling butterflies before her. Their colorful wings sparkled and won the rapt attention of the audience. They were so beautiful, one could scarce take her eyes off the pair even if they refrained from movement altogether. However, the strobe lighting cast by the firefly lighting crew certainly added to the couple's vast allure. It left a trail of luminosity that followed their every dramatic twist or turn. The two swallowtails held hands to begin their act with an initial bow. Then they nodded to E.Z. Hopper who picked up the tempo, now unmistakably a Latin beat. Immediately the two butterflies danced energetically, never once losing step with the other, as up and down the flowers they went. What grace! What elegance! The crowd cheered their tango. Why the only thing that came close in Cassandra's youthful imagination was an old black and white film starring the famed dance team Fred Astaire and Ginger Rodgers. To provide the grateful crowd with the fullest demonstration of their skills, E.Z. shifted tempos yet again. The butterflies ever so deftly altered gears to enact something of a cha cha cha. She wondered how each could move so quickly while simultaneously anticipating the other's steps? Perhaps they had danced together a long time? But to Cassandra's thinking, butterflies didn't actually live that long, which suggested something of a mystery. She was absolutely astounded by their performance, arguably her favorite thus far. When their number was completed, the male butterfly said, "Just a little something I picked up in Latin America." The crowd cheered. No one heard the female reply, "It only happens when I dance with you." However, Queen Buzz-bee seemed to pick up their cue!

The graceful butterfly dancers hit a nerve with the Queen, who let out a poignant sigh. It dawned on Cassandra that the royal one might be genuinely lonely. After all, for all her pomp and splendor, the Queen was conspicuously unaccompanied by a king. No one seemed to notice the Queen's change of mood besides Cassandra. The crowd was too riveted by the performances of the ultimately dynamic duo to allot due consideration to the Queen. The elegant pair followed up with a short encore dance number. Nonetheless when their entire electrifying performance came to an end, the crowd continued to cheer on and on. Perhaps the Queen subtly resented the tide of attention directed away from her; so she let out an unmistakable buzzing sound. Needless to say, it regained the crowd's attention she felt slipping away.

"I believe we shall take a break now for a short intermission," Queen Buzz-bee stated regally. Then she faced Cassandra who she apparently trusted enough to invest her confidence in, and stated privately, "I'm a hopeless romantic. I've just got to step out for a quick night flight. Can't help it, can I, if I have a thing for pilots?" The ladybugs in waiting began to gossip; and the word must have gone all the way down the line to the drones and worker bees dispersed beneath the Queen's royal lily-flower. The Queen surveyed her loyal servants from her lookout. Could she choose a worthy partner from so respectable a distance? And while Buzz-bee could barely hear the drones speaking below; Cassandra, so very tuned from the overload of recent conservations in fact did. One hardly tough and tumble drone said to his pal, "I just hope she doesn't choose me tonight. I am just SOOO not up for it!"

Queen Buzz-bee turned to Cassandra and said, "Would you excuse me, dear? Nature calls. It's the law of things, I dare say. For without li-bee-do, where would a bee be?" Leaving Cassandra to ponder that koan, the Queen was then readily escorted, practically lifted by her entourage in a descent down the flower. Once earthbound she began mixing among her faithful subjects, a number of hardly enthusiastic drones among them. It appeared that the royal one inspected the group for the one that held that special magnetism she hoped to engage. With all eyes on the Queen, Cassandra could not help overhearing a ladybug whisper to another, "Why of course no one wants to dance with the Queen! It's the kiss of death! Not one drone has EVER returned to speak of the encounter with certitude. Who wants to volunteer for THAT kind of service? It's not the date of any drone's dreams, I assure you!"

Nonetheless, Cassandra spied the Queen flying off with a male bee she had not yet had the pleasure to meet; and likely never would. Since an intermission had been called, Cassandra thought she would get up, stretch her legs, and walk around. It would be prudent to stop by and ask Ezekiel how he was doing. She had no idea what time it was; but the moon was luminous. Its fullness lit the sky. In a strange way the luminary seemed to watch the events just as she did. When she caught up with Ezekiel he seemed to be speaking straight into thin air. In spite of the moonlight it was difficult to discern the tiny forms of abounding insects that had gathered for the summer's best show.

"There she is!" Ezekiel stated to someone or something, as Cassandra approached. Before she had a chance to resolve the puzzle, Ezekiel said, "I'd like to introduce you to Radner."

Cassandra was not sure where to direct her focus, no less her words. Then she heard a high-pitched voice say, "Over here." It seemed that a little seed was speaking to her, not that that should seem any stranger than conversations with ants or grasshoppers. Turns out it was not one seed, but a trio of three pals who had elected, shall we say, to crash Queen Buzz-bee's party. Well, this would be a first. Ultimately that could be said about every one of Cassandra's most recent encounters!

Her attention was seized first by a rather adorable seed who assumed the shape of an acorn. He extended the tiniest hand you could ever imagine. "My name is Radner. My friends all think I'm a nerd just because I run the program of this seed." Then pointing at his two pals, he continued. "This is my best friend Nestor Nutworthy, and please don't call him nuts. It'll get him going on a tirade; and he'll never stop explaining why the whole world is nuts."

The nut, which is to say Nestor Nutworthy, wasted no time in cutting in to correct Radner's assessment. "I didn't say the whole world was nuts; I said it all began with nuts. What do you think all this (stated as he pointed to the trees surrounding their catered affair) started with?"

Not to be left out of the conversation, a little plant stood up on its roots to offer, "Hello. And pleased to meet you. I'm Irving the herb. Doctors run in my family. You could say medicine comes naturally to us; it's part of our filial line."

Cassandra was charmed by her new acquaintances. Ezekiel noted this fact yet decided to speed matters along, for who could predict when the Queen would return to resume the evening's scheduled performances? "Perhaps you'd like to show Cassandra inside?" He directed this comment at Radner.

"Oh. Yes. Yes. Certainly." Radner expertly used his thin tiny hand to unzip the front of his seed casing thereby exposing what could only be described as a sophisticated panel, not unlike those seen at airport terminals where traffic control officers direct planes to safe runways for landings. Cassandra was rather shocked. It never dawned on her that such high-tech equipment might reside inside the confines of a tiny seed casing.

"Your family owns a computer, isn't that right, Cassandra?" Ezekiel queried.

"Yes," she answered, not seeing where the question fit in with present circumstances.

"Well, the computer runs on tiny chips that house sophisticated codes. The seed you could say is the world's first organic computer chip. For it, too, holds a master code that sets out the blueprint for the entire tree that will eventually follow."

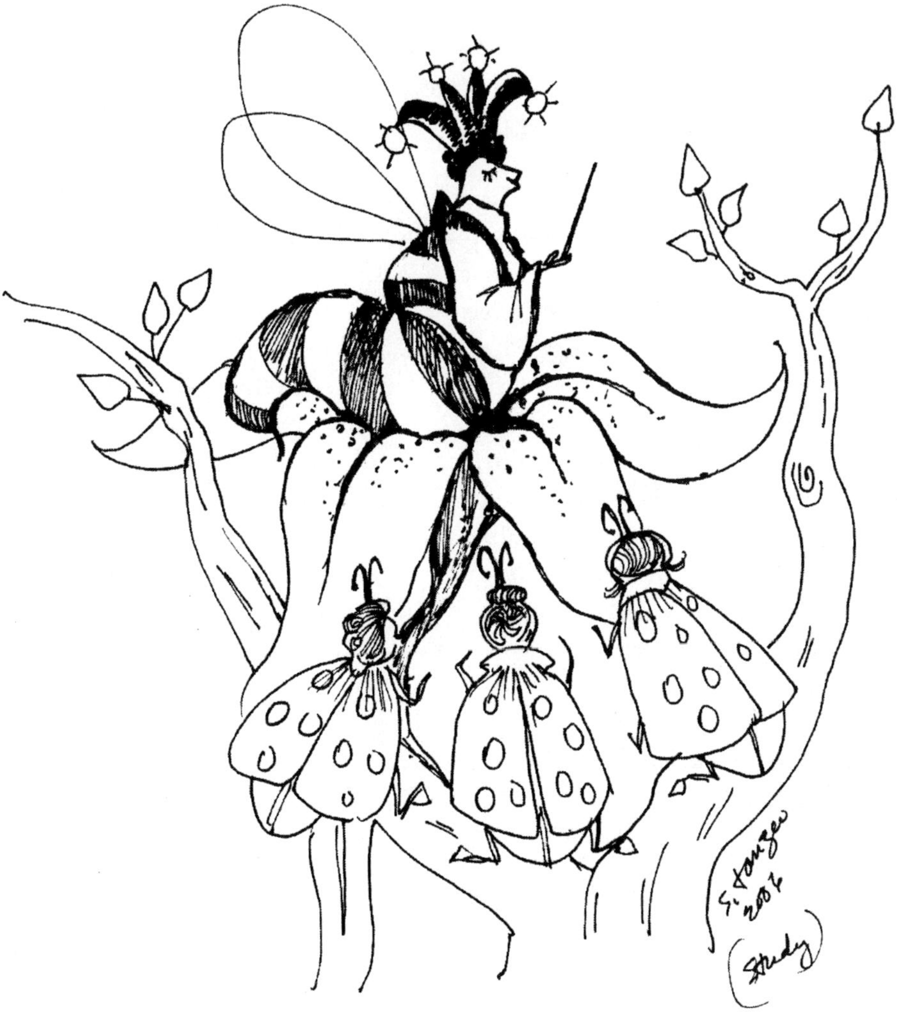

"Yeah, and it's a big job. I can't go slack or fall asleep at the wheel," Radner added. "I have to maintain the codes and tune the mechanisms to keep them running on course. I might as well have been a computer programmer! And trust me on this. You don't want to BE inside a hazelnut running THAT program! Talk about complicated!"

"Wow!" Cassandra said evidencing a clear sense of wonder.

"Wonder, ah yes. A good thing. And wonder is what you can count on encountering when taken under my wing, child; for indeed this is a wonder-filled world!" Ezekiel added with his customary zeal.

"I'll never look at a seed again and think it's just a simple thing," she added.

"More than that, we encourage you to go ahead and get your hands dirty! Plant a seed, or better yet, plant many! You will learn much from watching them grow." Those wise words were spoken by Radner and friends. Cassandra was glad to have met them; but just then she was fairly certain she heard a distinctive buzz in the air. Sure enough, the queen was just then bee-lining back to her lily perch. The ladybugs began to line up and assemble. And just as they had intimated, there was nary the shadow of a partner, pilot, or drone returned! Talk about ships passing in the night! But Cassandra was new to this world, and it was not hers to judge. Doing her utmost to honor polite protocols, she curtsied to the trio of new friends, and told Ezekiel she'd see him after the show. Then she made her way oh so carefully (so as not to squash any participants under foot) back to her pine crest seat of honor. Fortunately she took her seat just in the nick of time!

In her zeal she forgot to ask Ezekiel how he thought Grandfather was doing. "Go on and enjoy the show!" She heard the bird call back after her; and surprisingly he must have read her mind, for she also heard him say "You'll have time to consider him later." Then the parrot wisely grew silent, for the Queen had returned to her lily-throne.

Cassandra had no idea how late it actually was. She lost track due to her immersion in this tiny evocative world of intense sensory stimulation. Besides, she was too enthralled with the occasion to let time of any sort stand in her way. Meanwhile the Queen, being a queen, entertained not the slightest notion of informing the crowd of her recent date, or any future romantic plans. Therefore no mention was made of the drone now added to the unofficial list of missing bee-persons. Buzz-bee did however stage-whisper to Cassandra, "Alas! That was utterly refreshing. Now I feel regenerated; so let's get back to the show, shall we?" Having reclaimed her comfort zone, the royal one indicated that performances were ready to resume. She declared loudly: "Action. Camera? Take Two!"

A ladybug rushed to the Queen's side to whisper the name of the next upcoming act. And like clockwork, the Queen puffed up to relate the official announcement to the eager crowd. However, before the anticipated actors took center stage, Cassandra saw them approaching; and poor impolite thing, she just could not overcome the natural reflex to recoil. Fortunately in doing so she did not compromise the queen's balanced lily. Thankfully.

"And now for that mesmerizing act you all look forward to each year presented by Slish and his impeccably trained martial arts students, the Scorpios!" The queen bellowed with notable zeal. "Let's greet them with a round of applause."

Cassandra was utterly relieved to realize the scorpions were not headed her way; yet she could not help feeling intrigued by their magnetic stage-presence. Scorpions about to perform for a crowd! Could she believe her own eyes?

Slish, the largest of the scorpions, took center stage. Cassandra was curious as to how he got the patch worn so conspicuously over one eye. Was it for dramatic appeal, part of his costume perhaps? The ominous creature strutted about the stage ostensibly showing off his amazing albeit threatening tail. Then as if in answer to her unspoken question he introduced the upcoming act by first electing to share a didactic prologue.

"What you're about to witness will reveal far more than the eye can detect. We, members of the eighth ray are a mysterious kind, endowed by nature with a loaded weapon that we must learn to wield wisely for the entirety of our existences. As a young scorpion, I was proud; and it was my pride that led me into contests often of the lethal sort. Indeed, this patch bears witness to the lesson I learned. It remains an all too painful reminder. Yet it has taught me something valuable, something that I have passed on to my students. And it is this: that whoever masters himself, is greater than the one that elects to conquer a city. That realization came to me on the basis of the very real Initiation process that led to my wounds. Evidence speaks for itself: stung once is more than enough! It is wiser to resolve differences than live with the scars of bitter contention. Let me be clear in stating that too many of us mistake vengeance for justice. Indeed, I am living proof that these are not the same things. Strangely I have learned that silence can serve as a far more potent weapon than words uttered, or actions taken. Having said that, please join me in sharing the mastery of these young scorpion-performers. They will visually portray the fruit of the self-discovery process each has vigorously undergone. To impeccably execute difficult moves calls for a fearless examination of the motives that drive those actions. Dare to examine your own. It is our contention that the search for personal meaning constitutes a great and compelling mystery, one worthy of your lifetime's pursuit! And now may I proudly introduce The Scorpios!"

In perfect synchronicity four scorpions lifted to the stage. Each held his menacing tail to its fullest height and extension. Cassandra imagined to the tiny ants closely observing, these creatures would prove ominous if awesome! However, Slish had responsibly prepared the crowd for what they were about to observe; and it truly was every bit an art form. The scorpions each moved a step to the left, then an equally paced step to the right. As they repeated such moves each one brought his tail down where the other's deft motion left only empty space. E.Z. Hopper began shifting his drumming; and as the pace picked up, so did the quickness and alacrity of the scorpion's changing motions. In a strangely haunting way it seemed that each one was dancing with his own weapon. Their practiced graceful movements were distinctly designed NOT to hurt or attack what otherwise would have proven a ready opponent. The unusual nature of the choreography underway resembled Karate, or a related branch of the Martial Arts. Astute training in self-control was evident, for how much easier would it be to simply inflict the sting of direct impulse by striking one's partner? The dance the scorpions presented to the excited crowd portrayed a mastery of movement that triggered an important lesson by analogy. Cassandra found herself realizing that if a scorpion could control his reflex to strike out couldn't anyone else for that matter? When she gave that thought consideration, she realized that Slish was a teacher of the best possible sort.

At the end of their impressive routine, Cassandra could not be certain; but it seemed that a good number of insects in the audience gave them a standing ovation.

"Would you listen to all that applause coming from the crickets back there in the cheap seats!" E.Z. Hopper said loud enough for everyone to hear.

By this time Cassandra clearly recognized the sequence of protocols that followed beginning with a ladybug whispering again in the Queen's ready ear.

"Our next act is unique. It was inspired by our own musical director, E.Z. Hopper, who will be joined tonight by the lovely Beguila on harpsichord, along with the reclusive Sabius, on bass. They will present for the benefit of our honored guest Cassandra, a rendition of the Creation Allegory, a tribute to the Twelve Rays. Tonight's performance is an adaptation taken from the Writ to be executed in a jazz-rap hybrid. Let's give our talent a welcome round of applause, shall we?" The Queen baited the audience's hardly lapsing attention. Its ready enthusiasm was obviously on-tap!

Before the performers began to send their magic over the crowd, Cassandra asked Queen Buzz-bee, "What is the Writ?"

"Ah, yes. Good question. Sabius has constructed a concise compilation of the wisdoms gleaned from a number of sacred texts. If my memory serves me well, those sources include the Koran, the Kabbalah, the Torah, the Bible, the Upanishads; and frankly child, there may be others. But you really ought to pay attention now; for this is definitely not an act to be missed!"

Cassandra was appreciative of the Queen's astute explanation; and quite prepared to follow her advice. All eyes were cast upon the stage for what already looked to be a memorable performance. Then a guest from the audience yelled out, "Hit it, E.Z!"

Another voice echoed with, "Let it rip, Beguila!"

With a third yelling, "Get down, Sabius!"

The stately lime green, luminous praying mantis proved enchanting in his gentle gestures even before he began to strum the little gourd, probably strung by E.Z. Hopper's deft fingers. Beguila had woven tough new strands into her web, which when plucked by an experienced master, released the subtle tones of a melodic harp. Cassandra had the distinctive feeling that this number would prove to be a showstopper! And that was no easy task given the hypnotic thrill of the previously rendered performance. Talk about a tough act to follow!

Once the musical trio's melodious sounds began to blend, an invisible web wove itself around the audience. Its chief power was the capacity to alter mood. Everyone, including Cassandra, felt the ambiance turn dream-like. It was as if all present were suddenly transported to a distant planet with an atmosphere less dense than our own. Under the spell of this otherworldly setting, the hypnotic voice of Sabius guided the crowd of altered space explorers. The cadence of his utterances resembled those spoken in ancient parables. He assumed the cloak of timelessness, and spoke:

> "From the shores of time, when the world was nearly new
> Came a tribe of Twelve, from a distant starry avenue.
> And upon that very day
> All was transformed in the most magical way.
> For the great light of Creation split,
> Into twelve succinct rays, each with an intended gift.
> And so I introduce to you, in all humility,

The great circle of the twelve rays in their originality.
Utilizing Heaven's language, we hold the map to reach accords.
These express right relations, the means toward much reward.
To make of this design model a stunning success,
It has come time for us to share it with the rest.
Let it be known that Creator tried the experiment first on us;
Thus arriving at the pros, cons, kinks, and cogs proved a plus.
And that is how the twelve fundamental natures came to be.
There's one for you, and there's one for me.
Each ray a Creation of the one true light;
Everyone endowed with a special learning experience, that's right!
An intended Onederville with each of you a wonder;
With this new understanding, no need to further tear the world asunder.
We offer this great old news to you, so don't hesitate to tell another,
The world need not remain in darkness, it's time for all to discover
The secret essence: how the first twelve came to earth,
The miracle of every body's unique star-origin birth.
In this stellar understanding, all children may come to know
That earth is a marvelous living being; and you're ALL part of
her grandest show!"

Cassandra clapped vigorously, while crickets chirped. The Queen buzzed cheerfully; and a hundred other cacophonous sounds of gratitude issued forth from the animated crowd. Oddly so close to follow the thunderous applause did the first subtle hint of genuine thunder echo to signal a storm brewing somewhere in the distance that no one heard, or rather recognized its warning. Additionally, the loud crowd got so caught up in celebration, that its own self-generated uproar offset the sound of a deeper buzzing that was just then getting underway. It appeared to emanate from the ground beneath. How to describe it? It resembled the mantra-like reverberation of a hundred Buddhist monks chanting all together at once. The impact generated came upon the gentle gathering in recurrent waves. All merrymaking suddenly stopped, as the lively atmosphere was radically transformed into one of utter silence. Cassandra sensed the ominous change of humor. She listened intently to the whispers circulating around the crowd. What could account for this profound shift in attitude that every creature seemed to share at once? Since ladybugs in waiting were generally known for gossip; she wasn't sure if she could place trust in their accounts. Nor would it be prudent to seek out Ezekiel for the Queen had given no command for anyone to leave his seat. Furthermore, she feared she might bring an unfortunate creature to his premature demise should she step into the chaos of the crowd at this inopportune moment. It seemed that everyone held still while the dominant message passing from mouth to ear was: "We hope it's not them! Would they really show up to crash the party tonight, of all nights?"

Determining that as honored guest she had at least some rights and privileges, Cassandra could contain herself no longer. "Who are they?" She blurted out. The crowd practically hissed in response. No one seemed prepared to utter their name.

"They are about as much fun as vertigo at a rock climbing expedition," she heard an anonymous voice from the crowd answer. "Yeah. And they've got more baggage than a third world airport," she heard another say with unbearable cynicism. Apart from these speculations, the die was already cast. It was clearly too late. The echoing mantra had effectively opened the stones; and the very earth appeared to widen as a line of briefcase carrying, ledger holding, list-wielding resolute insects ascended. Each one exuded a sense of ominous authority that preceded his arrival aimed straight in front of the royal one. Apparently they knew exactly where they were headed. The scene reminded Cassandra of office workers in the downtown courthouse where she occasionally went with her mother to get important papers filed. "I never much liked dealing with bureaucrats," she could recall her mother saying. But Cassandra's flashback was rudely interrupted when the first one stepped forward to address the queen.

"Chronick 7714 honorable member of the tenth ray speaking. We are here to leverage a duty, your honor; for according to our records, we find there have been substantial discrepancies associated with your kingdom's last reported earnings."

Before the Queen could regain her composure, her dignity under fire in the midst of the season's proudest social event, a second seventeen-year locust in similar attire, not to mention demeanor, came forward.

"Chronick 11652 honorable member of the tenth ray speaking. I have this to add regarding your case; your majesty, what is your current rate status?"

"My what?" She answered with justifiable indignation. "Do you have any idea what it takes to run a hive like mine? How many dependents I have? Do you realize that members of the 5th ray provide financially uncompensated pollination services for one third of this country's entire agricultural system? Can you imagine the many mouths I have to feed in my own hive alone? Goodness, there are thousands of siblings! And tonight! Why this event happens to be a non-profit catered affair!"

"Chronick 11652 speaking. I will make note of these items in your file," he responded as dryly as a desert.

"My file?" She quipped with a tone of unmistakable righteousness.

Elektra, endowed with electrically acute powers of reasoning (as a member of the advanced eleventh ray) stepped forward. "What exactly are these alleged files for? And who gave you the authority to judge the Queen on the basis of said findings?"

Then Mr. Allura, distinguished counselor as member of the seventh ray came forward and directed his words toward the Queen. "Your majesty, if you require legal representation, I hereby extend my services. It would be my honor to represent you in association with these charges; gratis, of course. Pro bono is my specialty."

Beguila spun closer to get a clearer view of the action she had no intention of missing, and offered, "Plenty of important papers have been known to get lost in the web." She winked at the Chronicks before mischievously flipping over to show her dark intimidating side.

"Chronick 11652 speaking. Let me make something perfectly clear to each of you. All required dues are for your own protection, security, insurance and safety."

"Insurance? Security? Protection from what, when together we elect to resolve our differences and meet our challenges?" Elektra added brilliantly.

Cassandra was pretty riled up herself; after all, it was a great party and she didn't want to see it crashed. She owed that much to the Queen. And so she decided she'd also add her two cents. "Why is the Queen supposed to pay you guys, anyway?"

"Chronick 631111, honorable member of the tenth ray speaking. And who (he deliberately put Cassandra on the spot with his pointed words) might you be?" He then gestured to an assistant furiously trying to keep up with events by writing everything down, not unlike a court reporter, to add, "And make sure you note the presence of this outsider, Chronick 727258, would you?"

"My name is Cassandra. Queen Buzz-bee invited me here tonight as her honored guest; and I've been having a great time learning about the rays, and watching their talent show . . . until you came along!"

"Young lady, as we have prudently pointed out, we are members of the tenth ray; and as such, we wield a certain authority. We take it as no slight that we were not formerly invited to share in this occasion, for our job is a tough one. It falls on us to establish quality controls. Someone has to set a standard! We therefore track all the wrongs ever done, make sure the work gets done, that dues get paid, and inventions made. That each activity is up to code and executed in the proper mode. Do you think these demands make us popular?" His words struck Cassandra's tender heart for their sincerity.

"Well. I didn't think of all that." Cassandra politely responded.

"Chronick 72495, honorable member of the tenth ray speaking. And may I add that we must also make sure that all account for their precious time. Everyone has a purpose you know; and each of you also has allotted tasks to fulfill. Time, therefore, is not something to waste. Indeed it is something each must account for."

"Chronick 727258 speaking. Do you realize that well managed time can avert costly mistakes later? Why there is no better formula for quality control, no more cost-effective strategy available in all the world. And the key to this basic savings plan is to learn from your mistakes. We are here to make sure of that!" he added.

"Chronick 631111 speaking. I concur with the honorable Chronick 72495 and honorable Chronick 727258; for we are all members in good standing of the tenth ray, and therefore the formidable teachers of consequence."

"It's a good thing they only come back once every seventeen years," Elektra added flaunting her bold rebellious wit.

"Chronick 7714 speaking. You can be sure that WE hardly waste time down there! While a great many may wonder why we go missing for years at a time, it's due to the fact that there is countless data to register, record, collate and file. Then we must of course assess our findings. This in turn requires a formidable crosschecking of all factual information. Once it's done we must return again to update our records. I can assure you that we are thoroughly committed to our work, as you can deduce from our high professional standards."

"Chronick 72495 speaking. And we are not computerized yet."

"Good thing; or you might turn into SEVEN year locusts!" Elektra added for comic relief. The crowd let loose the considerable tension generated by this unwelcome encounter in the collective release of an outrageous giggle. (That is, as much as insects actually giggle.)

Seizing the occasion to expose his lighter side, Chronick 631111 announced himself; then broke pace to deploy a timely unexpected adaptation to public relations. What better way to win the crowd's heart, than with a song he reasoned? Without any formal introduction or announcement the locust let loose:

>"Should you begin to consider the pearl formed
> from a mere grain of sand,
> Or the exotic journey of a raindrop
> trapped in the cave of a distant land;
> Mixing over and across the centuries with mineral deposits,
> My goodness what results is the rarest of composites!
> I'm talking jewels, my friends, in point of fact.
> Time provides each with the opportunity
> to similarly upgrade his act!"

"Bravo," raved the Queen, never realizing that a group as stiff as the tenth ray might harbor artistic inclinations. Nor was she offended by the impromptu performer who bypassed her royal permission by rendering his act unannounced. The Queen was in surprisingly good humor as she turned to face the Chronicks and say, "Why don't you just stay, relax, and enjoy the remainder of our party. We'll be passing out the Golden Honey Awards shortly. By the way that's another write-off for your accountant to make note of," she teased.

"Yeah. Lighten up," Elektra added, "No one's got you guys on the clock now; so quit being so darned serious!"

Perhaps the dramatic turn of events stirred the Queen's passions. For suddenly, without prelude or introduction, she began to bellow out a tune of her own.

"This one's for all of you." She said, gracefully, while eyeing the Chronicks in particular. Then she began:

>"We all readily acknowledge that . . .
>To be a bee, or not to be a bee, that is the question.
>For one can BEE witty; one can BEE charming,
>One can BEE generous, or ultimately disarming;
>But the key, is to really BEE yourself,
>For where would this world BEE without you?
>So BEE novel! BEE inventive. BEE here now;
>and by all means enjoy the show!"

The bee then took her seat, and was fanned by appreciative ladybugs in waiting. She fully intended to chill; but the crowd's cheer went on and on; and that only meant one thing: time for an encore!

Cassandra, however, had something troubling her mind and didn't think it would be rude to pose the question, or speak out of turn. She bluntly stated in something that amounted to a challenge to the queen: "I thought it was to BE or not to be?"

Apparently taken aback by the youngster's spirited pitching of her own flawed but otherwise bold literary savoir-faire, Buzz-bee responded:

"Alas, child. That is the edited version!" And then yielding to the crowd's incessant call for more; she burst into song a second time, as if to sing out her very robust heart and soul.

> "Never tell a bee how to bee!
> They say I've got dues to pay . . .
> When what I do's, I only do's for love!
> Who could put a price on the priceless?
> Gracious! That would become anyone's guess!"

And then with a mesmerizing synchronicity that left the crowd wondering if the two had planned this duet from the start, Guido got back on stage and sent plaintive song-lines straight toward the Queen. She in turn answered his lyrics with remarkable Broadway style. What a lively duet they made!

> "Time is like a rock. Forever it goes round,
> Everything comes full circle. Just look around." Guido bellowed.
> "Consider a nest, or a mature lady's breast;
> The child in the womb, the moth's cocoon."

The Queen responded. Then together they chanted in unison:
> "Planets each orb, revolve, and spin . . .
> The circle of life is what we're in.
> Time is a circle, that's round like me.
> If you look back far enough, the future will become a distant memory."

Guido offered the last lyric, and it sent the crowd into a frenzy of appreciation. Hearing the welcome cheers The Queen blew several kisses to her fans, profusely thanked Guido, and quickly turned to Cassandra to ask in a careful whisper, "Do you think I have a weight problem? I can't seem to contain this roundness bout the middle. It's job related, of course. I do my utter best; but it falls upon me to put all that delectable honey to the test." The crowd seemed to wait upon the Queen's next pronouncement, or song. Since she so loved center stage, the Queen took to the spotlight rather naturally. Nonetheless she needed to pause momentarily to compose herself before resuming lest she risk breathlessness. Although tonight she was prepared to give it her all! So up she rose from her lily to let loose yet again!

> "To make this world a sweeter place
> Takes all my strength, the sum of grace.
> And yet I wonder at the oddest of times
> Given the expanse of my kingdom, so sublime,
> What life would be like if I had a king . . .
> Would I be up on this stage, would the crowd hear me sing?
> Would I ever and always find myself on the run,
> Catering to his wishes, the honey-making never done?
> If I had to listen for his every demand,
> What of centuries of my own feminine command?"

The crowed cheered. Cassandra clapped vigorously; and the Chronicks seemed to be having the time of their lives, too.

"And now may I announce my absolute favorite, and the evening's grand finale: 'The Waltz of the Mantid Moon'." At the sound of those intriguing words, E.Z. Hopper hit the drums, Beguila got back on her harpsichord, and Guido picked up a reed-flute. What a trio of virtuosity this lively group made!

With the moon still high in the sky, although clouds had started to secretly gather, seven tall luminous Praying Mantises at once filled the stage. The Termites had planned accordingly for there was just enough space to accommodate this troupe. After all, they towered over most of the other guests. In exquisite synchronicity, the seven began doing what Cassandra later learned were ancient movements known as Tai Chi. It seemed they all entered into a trance state; and it was a marvel to watch them move together as if one singular organism. It truly enchanted the audience as their long elegant arms and ever so trim legs lifted into the air, then came down slowly and gracefully. Certain moves were repeated, while others were painstakingly elaborated upon. It was nothing short of a majestic vision to behold; and Cassandra cherished the rare experience.

It was at this time that a discernible burst of thunder was ostensibly heard. The Queen bee recognized that a higher authority was speaking. She knew that it would be wise to speed up the ceremony, and tie things up before any burst of rain or yet worse weather befell them. For indeed weather had become something of a dangerous anomaly for all creatures, great and small in recent years. Besides, as any good leader knows, responsibility for protecting the diverse flock fell to her.

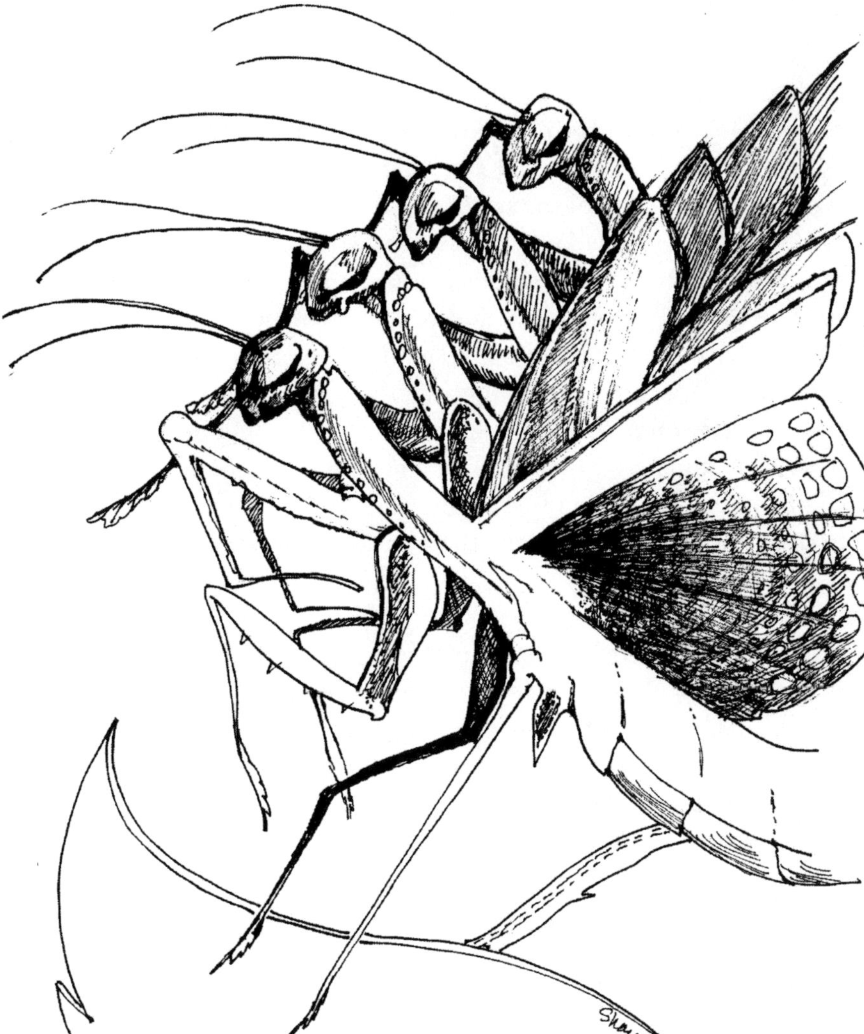

A sterling round of applause followed the dancing mantises in their dazzling performance. It was clearly time for the royal bee to pass out the coveted awards. Cassandra spied the worker bees moving through the crowd carrying the glowing sculptures, each rendered in amber in the image and likeness of a chubby bee.

Just before the Queen began to announce the show's winners and pass out the awards, a shy roach, notably related to the one Cassandra conversed with in Grandfather's kitchen, came forward with a radiant piece of gold. Granted passage she humbly presented the object to the Queen.

"While my kind, members of the fourth ray, tend to prefer home and hearth to the bright lights of the stage, one thing we are adept at is collecting objects of value. So on behalf of my ancestors, who hail back to the very tombs of Egypt, may I present you with this golden scarab." She passed the jeweled ornament to the very appreciative and equally surprised Queen bee.

"My heavens, darling. I just love gold! What a thoughtful gift; fit, I might add for a Queen!" Naturally the crowd burst into joyous applause with those warm words. "Let me thank all our guests for coming out tonight. You give me so much. Yet I am already endowed with the greatest of these, which is love. For it deeply satisfies my heart to be so naturally gifted and able to make honey that sweetens the world for all. It also happens to be good karma."

The crowd laughed.

"Alas, the time has come, and the privilege is all mine, to pass out tonight's awards. Let me say that each of you is a winner whether your talents are acknowledged on the stage this blessed evening, or otherwise. For we all benefit when we gather in this manner to share our talents. As a natural patron of the arts, I recognize the vital importance of events like this. Oh, how I love show biz! How fortunate we are to have among us so diverse a body of entertainers, and this rich venue perfect for the cross-pollination of novel ideas and inspiration. A ceremony of this order encourages us all to grow and evolve. What a Divine plan! And now as constituted by a recipe that's been in my family for ages, kissed as it were by the warm bliss of the sun, and spun into the substance of liquid gold: The Golden Honey Awards!" She paused to both catch her breath and direct the comment at a member of the 10th ray. "Write that down Chronick number 88-007 wherever you are. I am privileged to now present the following: For best performance in the execution of astute stage lighting . . ." She waited for a Ladybug in waiting to present her with an envelope. "And the award goes to Elektra and company, members of the eleventh Ray!"

The delighted fireflies flew up, and did their utmost to awkwardly fly off carrying the heavy golden honey award along with them.

Cassandra heard a ladybug whisper, "They always get that one."

"And now, for best performance by an insect couple, in the art of dance . . ." Once again, a ladybug arrived with the appointed envelope. "The award goes to the Alluras!" The crowd cheered for certainly each unique talent deserved due credit. The lovely butterfly couple collected their award and offered a modest pirouette in gratitude.

"And next. For best performance by a ray in the art and execution of musical direction, the award goes to . . ." Yet again, a ladybug presented the necessary envelope, so the Queen could formerly announce, E.Z. Hopper as the winner.

E.Z. Hopper, Cassandra had already noted did not have much use for modesty. As she might have expected he took full advantage of his moment of recognition. The fireflies did their part to lend him the spotlight. He held his Golden Honey Award up high and spoke these words in rap:

"I accept this award on behalf of the ninth ray.
It's no secret that my kind invented rhythm to fill the night air.
Song's been created to reverberate everywhere.
Just ask the birds in those high treetops,
They'll tell you quite plainly who invented bee bop!"

Then the Queen resumed her role as master of ceremonies, and went on with the award ceremony. "Always a crowd pleaser, allow me to present the award for best performance by an insect in the art of catering . . ." A ladybug hurried over with the envelope. "And the award goes to our own Fifi Alfredo." The crowd cheered. And once again Cassandra heard a whisper among the ladybugs in waiting, "Oh. She always gets that one, too!"

As the award process continued, Cassandra sensed her thoughts drifting back to the cottage. She wondered how Grandfather's little research party was going. What she didn't know was that the last peal of thunder had roused him from his laboratory; and like all good, concerned Grandfathers he decided to check in on her . . . and Ezekiel. But to his surprise, she was not to be found, at home that is. His sense of indignation was pronounced once he faced the shocking finding that his trusted bird had likewise abandoned his cage to disappear! Something was rotten in Denmark, and he would waste no time in getting to the bottom of it! Quickly the research party morphed itself into an ad hoc search party! Luckily for Cassandra, the unlikely trio was not up to speed. Had there been a serious thunderstorm on the move, intended rescue efforts would have been thwarted by the excessive energy the group needlessly expended in securing a number of presumably necessary items and related paraphernalia. By the time the troupe was ready to stake out the place in search of the thought lost girl, they had amassed mosquito netting, several rival brands of bug spray, flashlights, raincoats, a compass, and even an unwieldy umbrella. The professor, Millicent and Dr. Quackenbush diligently surveyed the entire property surrounding the cottage. Up until this time the Professor was absolutely certain that Cassandra could be nowhere else; after all, he presumed that the back gate was still safely padlocked. Little did he know!

"What in carnation would drive that child out on a night like this?" He asked rhetorically of his colleagues. "This is North Florida! There are snakes, alligators, wild pigs, even panthers out here! Doesn't she know better?" He added with justifiable fear and trepidation. By this time, Millicent was none too pleased to find herself exposed to 'the elements' and wished the boys would excuse her. She was a lady, after all, and not dressed for the ill-fated occasion. Her skirt, stockings, and sensible pumps were no match for the undergrowth of sticks, branches and unruly vegetation. This was most certainly NOT the research assignment she had signed up for. However, she did not want to appear indifferent to Cassandra's well-being; so she bravely carried on. When all logical deductions and practical solutions failed them, efforts were further impeded by the fact that they began to argue vehemently among themselves like the *Three Stooges*! Having run out of rational options with the object of their inquiry still quite missing; there was no choice but to make way to the property line and inspect the status of the back gate. The flashlight revealed what the Professor had great difficulty accepting: someone had picked the lock! It was as if a prizefighter had punched him right in his gut. To say that he was crestfallen would prove a gross understatement. Still, with a dangerous storm front due to arrive at any moment, he could not afford to indulge his compromised emotions.

"I knew that bird knew a lot more than he let on in conversation! I should have left him with the pirates!" Erroneous stammered!

"Now Erroneous, it's rather poor strategy to focus on blame right now. There's a storm brewing and we've got a youngster, and possibly a renegade bird to find before things get out of hand. Your Granddaughter probably has no idea how quickly the weather can change here in the Florida peninsula."

"Hush! Felix. Don't say such things," Millicent added. "Don't you know you'll worry the professor even more? At least it's apparent where that bird learned those nasty profanities!"

The professor, preferring to forget the shameful words uttered earlier by his previously loyal pet returned the group's concentration to the more troubling matter at hand. "Well. They must be out here somewhere!" His forecast was rendered in words of measured gravity. "This is no place for a child, especially on a stormy night; but at least we are well prepared for every exigency." He referred of course to the intolerable gear they dragged along on their little safari.

As the small group made their way through the gate towards the pond, the professor luckily took a wrong turn. As fate would have it, this fortuitous development meant that Cassandra would be privileged to participate in the evening's closing activity. The mood radically shifted as Queen Buzz-bee's bash succumbed to the first flashes of lightning seen in the sky. The insects knew what this sign meant. It would not be long before they would need to seek cover. Just before the party disbanded, Ezekiel summoned his most melodic voice, reminiscent of what one would expect from one of his relatives, the songbirds. He spoke first with humor; then altered his tone to one of solemnity.

"I guess you're wondering why I called this meeting here tonight?"

Had there not been the intimation of dangerous storm clouds breeding above, his comedy act would have likely won greater applause. Instead the Queen did what Queens did best. She offered a rebuff.

"Cut to the chase, big bird . . . this heavy sky will not long hold; and I must secure the safety of all members of my hive, not to mention the circle. So get on with it, will you!"

"Indeed I shall. Since all twelve rays are here assembled, it presents an apt opportunity to offer each of you a special gift; while at the same time apprising my favored student of a marvelous demonstration." With those tempting words, Ezekiel managed to hop down and quickly secure a slim stick quite similar to the pointer he deftly used in the elemental classes shared with Cassandra at that very spot. "Now it's quite evident to each of you that your designated ray was designed to fulfill certain quite specific functions. Indeed, each of you holds a key facet to this great puzzle called life. The circle reveals a marvelous plan virtually written into the heavens. In addition, it's nonsectarian, non-racist, non-sexist and non-partisan," and then turning to the Queen, he queried, "Did I leave out anything?"

Queen Buzz-bee just responded with an impatient stare.

"Put plainly, your little group represents a set of cosmic cousins by the dozen. And as for that gift I mentioned, I am hereby authorized by a certain winged dignitary to dub each of you with his stellar title." Ezekiel hobbled over to R. Killies and with the slender stick protruding from his mouth, he struck it lightly on first the left and then the right shoulder of the proud fire ant. "I dub thee R. Killies, ambassador of the first ray, and emissary for the sign of Aries. You are hereby guardian to April's children from all across the world, their teacher of personal courage." He moved on to Guido, and following the same ritual stated, "And I dub you, Guido, ambassador of the second ray, emissary of the sign of Taurus. You are equipped to teach May's children worldwide, the art of securing foundation." Sensing that time was of the essence, Ezekiel hurried over to Beguila, who had woven a little something just for the occasion. He reached up to tap her shoulders extra gently. "I dub you, Beguila, ambassador of the third ray, Gemini. You hereby are officially authorized to teach the world's June babies the ways, means, and benefits to informed communication." Next he moved on to Concha. Repeating the ritual he stated, "And to you Concha, ambassador of the fourth ray, I dub thee Cancer. It goes to you to prepare the world's July-born children for close family bonding." Knowing when a bit of theatrics, and/or flattery was due, he ventured closer to Queen Buzz-Bee. "And you, your royal highness, I dub thee Guardian of the fifth ray, ambassador to the sign of Leo. How well you fulfill your task in passionately expressing the desires of the healthy generous heart. Guide the August-born youngsters to follow their most golden impulses." He barely touched the Queen for he did not care to risk offending her and coming to know her reputable sting too intimately. Next he deftly proceeded to Sister Tee. "And on behalf of Nutra, Tidy-up, and the others, I dub you all members of the sixth ray, ambassadors of the sign of Virgo. You are granted the roles of teaching healing, service, order and efficiency to September's children."

By this time Grandfather must have recognized his error, for the little trio was now gaining on the assembled Star Circle. Even Ezekiel sensed their pending arrival. He did his best to speed up the dubbing process.

On to the Alluras, he dubbed them Libra, guardians of the seventh ray. "And to you both go the blessed task of inspiring balanced union in the October born." Slish hardly presented the easiest of candidates to approach; but Ezekiel had pledged to not only show Cassandra the full assembly of the twelve rays but also educate her with respect to their unique individual missions. He gingerly approached the large scorpion, and very gently used the stick to tap his shoulders. "I dub thee Scorpio, ambassador of the eighth ray. And to you goes the special task of inspiring rebirth, regeneration and transcendence in November's children that they learn to forgive their own, as well as others' trespasses." E.Z. Hopper could hardly wait for his turn to arrive. Ezekiel tapped his eager shoulders and anointed him Sagittarius, ambassador of the ninth ray. "And to you, E.Z. Hopper, goes the task of inspiring positive outcomes, as you teach December's children to focus their intentions accordingly." The Chronicks had hardly counted on receiving any gifts for their evening's troubles; but had taken their rightful place in the circle. Ezekiel approached the most accessible one, not bothering to discern one from the other based on their numerical designations. He wisely intended to expedite matters for he sensed that the weather had only extended them a temporary grace period. This kind reprieve was to ensure that they finish their ritual. "And you, honorary members of the tenth ray, are hereby dubbed Capricorn; and you are to provide January's youngsters with the drive to own personal achievement and accountability." He tapped a firefly hovering close to the activities, and said, "Dear, dear Elektra, representative of the eleventh ray, I dub thee Aquarius; and you shall guide February's children to invention, and inspire their discovery process." And just as the sagacious parrot approached Sabius, a whistle sound was heard. Many of the insects took off both in fear of the weather and the now closely approaching intruders. Cassandra, however, waited patiently as she very much wished to see the full circle drawn to its natural conclusion. It was an education of the truest sense to come to understand each of the participants, not to mention his higher purpose. Speaking so fast his words condensed into nearly unintelligible gibberish, Ezekiel tapped Sabius. "I dub thee, Sabius, ambassador of the twelfth ray, Pisces. And it is yours to guide the children of March to compassion. They are in this world to evidence concern for all others." Suddenly an owl hooted. It was an appropriate omen for just then Grandfather arrived on the scene. His sense of shock radiated like a siren. He was stunned to the point of mortified to find his dutiful Granddaughter and trusted pet bird, in the middle of a small field, apparently deserted. It was improbable that they should be out there at all 'round midnight. Instinct had duly alerted Cassandra's novel companions now safely removed from the threat of being sprayed to death. All had evacuated in the nick of time. Though none were present, Erroneous fogged the absent air, just in case. Cassandra didn't know what she could possibly say to change his attitude, and therefore elected to remain speechless. Getting busted was hardly fun! Just at that instant, as fate would have it, a huge crack of thunder let loose; and Ezekiel couldn't miss the opportunity to say, albeit under his bird breath, "Saved by the bell!"

The half-angry, half-relieved Professor looked up at the equally wrathful sky and said, "I need not tell you that you will have an awful lot of explaining to do once we get back to the safety of the cottage; but it's not worth getting struck by lightning to argue out here in this storm. Heaven's, child, what got into you?"

Cassandra half-hoped that Ezekiel would come to her rescue; but the bird had lived with the professor long enough to know when silence would prove more effective than words. He would prepare his explanation in due time.

Millicent, on the other hand, exhausted from the search and overwhelmed by her ill-equipped exposure to the elements, could hardly wait to get back to the cottage. The evening took a turn she scarcely had anticipated, nor would she care for a repeat performance ever again. Cassandra, in contrast, cherished every moment of the night's assorted encounters, each an original, to be sure. Having been formerly introduced to all twelve rays she could scarce share her unusual findings with her grandfather, at least not now. She would however lay out vivid descriptions in her journal before she forgot a single amazing thing. One thing the professor had not thought to take among his provisions was a cage; therefore Ezekiel was by all accounts still free. While he would have preferred trekking back on Cassandra's now welcome and familiar shoulder; that was not what the professor had in mind. Erroneous extended his arm like a command; and without needing to utter a single word the parrot complied. Felix tried to lift the group's spirits, but everyone was too exhausted to respond. It was a case of heavy gravity! So silence proved the best medicine as the four made their way back to the cottage with rain profusely falling.

Once safely returned to their lodgings, the first thing the professor did was lock Ezekiel into his cage. This time he placed the key in his own jacket pocket while staring intently at his Granddaughter. Millicent, in an attempt to neutralize the strained mood said, "I think I'll put up some tea. I'm sure we could all use a hot cup of tea after being exposed to the elements. And thank heavens we missed the worst of it." Just as she filled the teakettle with water, the roof echoed the repeated beatings of a hard rain now briskly falling. Cassandra asked if she could please be excused to change into dry clothing. Then she promptly returned, and took it as a small blessing that the group had decided to stay for tea, thus preventing her Grandfather from any strident interrogations. In the most demure fashion she could summon, given the night's adventure, she sipped her tea as quiet as a mouse.

It wasn't long before both Millicent and Dr. Quackenbush emptied their cups. As they prepared to leave, Dr. Quackenbush tapped his long-time friend Erroneous gently on the shoulder, "Why don't you let it wait till morning. I'm sure she'll be able to explain matters better after a good night's sleep."

The professor was apparently too strained to either debate the matter, or answer. He merely nodded. Cassandra used the pause for her own strategic escape. Without daring to approach him for a goodnight kiss, she instead looked back at him as she began to walk toward her room, and stated with gentle tenderness, "Goodnight, Grandfather. Sweet dreams." And then she blew him a kiss.

It was not a night she would ever forget. Still, she was out like a light the moment her head hit the pillow. Sleep would carry her back to the festivities where she could relive the best of the twelve rays' performances in her dreams!

PEACEMAKING FORCES

When the glare of the sun woke Cassandra the following morning, she knew she would soon have to face the music. Listening for any stir of Grandfather about the house, she began her bathroom routine, washed up, and came to the empty kitchen to utter a sigh of relief. Apparently the professor had resumed his laboratory work. He was nowhere to be seen. Perhaps his findings had not proven as firm as he led himself to believe prior to his colleagues' review? Or was it that he sought refuge away from the chaos of the emergency rescue operation that dominated the fateful night before? Cassandra was too young to realize that research provided a form of therapy for the usually calm, even-keeled gentleman. It soon became clear that he had elected to go to his personal sanctuary to secure the wisdom that would guide him before confronting his prized Granddaughter with the burden of his justifiable disappointment. All Cassandra knew was that it felt like a reprieve, an advantageous time to meet with her "defense attorney," Ezekiel, who also happened to be an accessory to the crime as perceived by Grandfather. Cassandra was too nervous to feast on granola until the two had a chance to discuss plans, if not a tenable strategy!

"While I would no doubt prefer to review with you the lessons and high points of last night's rather scintillating gathering; our cause du jour consists of formulating a united defense." No sooner had Ezekiel stated his objective, and begun to layout the plan, did the professor, pale as a ghost enter the kitchen. His mood was brusque. He intended to waste no time and indeed he cut right to the chase.

"Young lady, I need not tell you how disappointed I am in your conduct. I realize I have been very lenient with you this summer; but there ARE rules to follow on my premises; rules that exist for a very good reason: safety! You know better than to venture out into the wilds where dangers lurk! So, to make sure no such transgressions ever happen here again, a professional locksmith will arrive later today to install a lock he assures me cannot be broken! And furthermore, Ezekiel will remain confined to his cage at all times. Is that understood?"

"Yes, Grandfather." Cassandra responded, cowering under the weight of his authoritarian words. Ezekiel, possessed of a considerate soul could not bear the child's leaden sense of guilt, nor did he feel blameless in the matter. He had no choice then but to blow his cover. If ever there was a time to teach an old bird, that is to say, the professor, new tricks, it was then and there. Necessity called for innovation, if not downright invention!

"Now see here Professor! If one does not venture where they've never been, how can they come to know what they're yet to discover?"

The professor was so taken aback by the logical articulation emanating from the bird that he had to sit down, lest he lose all sense of his once balanced senses!

Seizing the advantage, Ezekiel continued. "Since you have seen fit to spend all your time in the laboratory, the education of Cassandra has largely fallen to me. No apologies necessary; and please do not interrupt. These words of explanation are long overdue. For I have observed you closely over the years, and am therefore positioned to speak with candor as I relate the empirical evidence acquired. And it is thus: Old ways of thinking and beholding the world have brought current events to shall we say a crisis. Therefore in my view it would be disingenuous, not to mention disastrous, to expect your Granddaughter, and her entire generation for that matter, to replicate what clearly is not working! Put plainly, Professor, you do not have all the answers! If you did war, poverty, suffering, disease and environmental abuse would not prove the debacles they have indeed become! In point of fact, human beings have much to learn in the ways and means to becoming better neighbors to nature's considerable kingdoms. Alas, yes. I said kingdoms. Furthermore, since I happen to share this world, I have a compelling interest in the proper education of those positioned to inherit it. They may yet come to improve upon things. Was it not your own respected scientist Einstein who stated, 'No problem can be solved at the level of thinking that brought it about?' And that is precisely where I come in; for in sharing my bird's eye view of the world, I have elected to guide the lovely Cassandra beyond linearity, to broaden her thought process so as to embrace, shall we say, the full circle. Therefore I implore you to impose no punishment on Cassandra. I take full responsibility for last night's matter; and offer this lengthy explanation that I might bring the light of truth to bear upon the mistake you would otherwise believe she alone has conceived and committed." To say that the Professor was stun-gunned would be putting it mildly. However before Grandfather could recover his wits now blown somewhere off into the cosmos on account of the bird's expansive intellectual delivery, Ezekiel continued. "And furthermore, another useful thing worth noting is that it's often true that mystics, artists, poets and the like have seen what science, or should I say scientists have not. Take for instance the work of cubism as executed by visionary painters before the turn of the 20th century? Did they not break the planes of matter well in advance of your physicists? Would that the latter had used their discovery for so peaceful a cause as the artists! I say there is something valuable to be learned from the voices your so-called experts have seen fit to silence for too long."

Temporarily unable to offer so much as a word of response, the Professor got up. It seemed that was all he could do. He then thrust himself outside in pursuit of the fresh air his survival urges led him to believe would prove his only hope for clearing or otherwise regaining a mind he now believed utterly lost. Given his age and lifelong line of reasoning, he just could not take in the apparent phenomenon of a parrot apprising him of the facts of life, or otherwise reading him the riot act!

Suddenly a silent witness emerged who had listened to the entire conversation from behind the kitchen wall. Cassandra recognized the intruder as Concha. "Goodness, gracious!" The empathetic roach stated. "I just peeked in to make sure you got back alright last night. That was quite a storm."

"Oh, did you get caught in the rain?" Cassandra responded thoughtfully.

"I didn't mean THAT storm, I meant this one." As an unofficial member of the household, Concha sensed the domestic turbulence permeating every nook and cranny of the Professor's home; and she thought she could offer some helpful advice. "One thing I've learned is to trust my instincts. When I sense danger looming, I know it's wise to stay out of harm's way. After all, not everyone treats us like family; and while I hate to admit it, for home is everything to us, we are simply not welcome in a great many domiciles. On the other hand what's clear to me is that everyone is looking for the perfect home. My dear mother told me 'if you get a good address, the world will give you credit for the rest.' And it's evident that people have moved about in search of that goal ever since the great flood! Now in your particular case, if you can't escape confrontation; there are proven ways to defuse it. How you rightfully might ask? By telling Grandfather he's right, and that you will respect his wishes from here on in because he IS your Grandfather. Listen to me! I know a thing or two about family matters as an official representative of the fourth ray. Of course Ezekiel's philosophy is right in many ways; but we must remember that blood is thicker than water. What your Grandfather needs right now is the assurance of your trust, not a scientific explanation. Go child. Comfort him. Do the right thing."

Cassandra gazed up at Ezekiel and said, "Well. It was your idea to introduce me to the twelve rays. Seems to me someone said never to presume there is only one right way to see, when the twelve rays present outright diversity. So I happen to think you're both right; but for now I'm going to follow Concha's recommendation." With those confident words, Cassandra left Ezekiel, now officially on house arrest, and walked out the front door hoping to comfort her Grandfather. She did not hear Ezekiel parrot back, "Did I say that? I don't remember saying that?"

Silently the young girl slipped up behind the crestfallen scientist who was seated on a weathered patio chair. She gently placed her hands on both of his shoulders in an approach that was natural and instinctive "I'm sorry if I disappointed you, Grandfather," she said with a tenderness that could melt the hardest heart.

Smart enough to realize that sustained hurt feelings were too high a price to pay for his need to be right, he placed his hand atop one of Cassandra's. "Granddaughter, I have no desire to be a tyrant; and I have yet to take in the indictment levied against me by that most unusual of birds; but I do know that my actions represent my obligation to your parents to protect you from harm." Then orienting as best he could to face the child, he continued, "I still do not know what possessed you to hazard such evident dangers in last night's unfortunate quest?" When it looked like Cassandra would not provide an answer any time soon, his quick mind came up with a compromise. "I seem to recall that there were a number of seed varieties purchased not long ago; and I believe this episode marks the perfect opportunity to put them to good use. We shall make our amends in planting a garden together. How does that sound?"

"It sounds very good, Grandfather. There's just one thing." She hesitated, not sure it was a good time to bring up yet another potentially explosive issue.

"And what might that be, child?" He asked respectfully.

"I don't want to spray any poisons on the garden."

"How then would you protect it from the ravages of the varied and sundry insects that would otherwise override not only your garden, but the entire property?"

Arriving at a bold idea she recognized where she could use her Grandfather's respect for science in concert with the furthering of her preferred course. "Grandfather, what if we tried a little experiment?" She asked, knowing full well she had extended a lure he could hardly resist.

"An experiment, did you say? What exactly would it consist of?" He responded.

"Well. We would prepare the yard for not one, but two gardens because they need to be separated. In my garden, I will plant seeds and tend to them in my own way; and in your garden, if you absolutely must use pesticide, then you will only use it on YOUR portion."

"I fail to see where the experiment comes in, Granddaughter?"

"An experiment is done in order to see results, right?" She asked. "So if your garden turns out to grow better than mine, then your methods win. But honestly Grandfather, I hope they don't!" Suddenly she was seized by strong emotions as her novel bond with the twelve rays animated her sense of protectiveness towards them. "If all your poisons work, there'll be nothing left! Everything will be as flat and boring as dirt!"

Not only had the professor never thought of his work in that way before, he was genuinely moved by his Granddaughter's feelings. He could not quite grasp why she seemed absolutely adamant against the use of what to him were miracle products; but after Ezekiel's earlier diatribe, his worldview had been permanently thrown off kilter. As a result, there were a great many things revolving around in his once firm made up mind.

"All right, then," he said, stroking his Granddaughter's head. "We shall have an experiment; and I dare say it will begin today!"

Cassandra rushed at him with a hug that nearly threw him further off balance.

"I must see to it that we have within our midst the necessary accoutrements for the task: such things as shovels, gloves, and . . . well, I suppose you will not wish to protect yourself with any bug spray?"

"No. I will wear pants and a long-sleeved shirt. I even have a hat!" Cassandra evidenced a ready enthusiasm for the challenge she had personally designed. "Build the garden and they will come," she mused to herself sensing she would need the help of her insect friends to win this contest with her Grandfather. In the meanwhile, the two pioneers got down to work, removing sticks, clearing weeds, and preparing the ground for a twin set of experimental harvests.

A RETURN TO THE GARDEN

It seemed that no sooner did Cassandra actually start planting her seeds, that Nutra, Tidy-up, and even Sister Tee (and a cast of at least one hundred other members of the sixth ray) came by to inspect the progress of her labors.

"I'm beginning a garden. Right now I'm planting the seeds," Cassandra explained.

"So we gathered," answered Tidy-up.

"And we implore you not to use any herbicides, pesticides or insecticides." Nutra offered her studious advice in an ominous tone. "People are much healthier we have noticed when they eat au natural; and there's no better way to do that then to grow your own produce."

"Fruit of the garden, it's been done since the beginning of time," Sister Tee added.

"Since your kind started cultivating the land," Tidy-up clarified.

"If you take the time to plant a seed and then nurture its growth along the way; one day it will return the favor and nourish you!" Sister Tee said with demonstrable mirth.

"That's precisely why we recommend your not making poisons a part of your harvest; for if you do, they will soon become a part of you." Scary albeit honest words were spoken by Nutra.

"We know all about your Grandfather's laboratory, and how tempting it must be to think you can spray one chemical here, and another there, and think pronto! Presto! All problems are solved." Tidy-up offered further.

"I wasn't planning to use ANY chemicals!" Cassandra said in her own impressive defense. "Actually, you could say that I've put Grandfather and his scientific methods to the test. We have officially begun a contest."

"That sounds interesting. Tell us more?" Nutra asked with all due respect.

"Well, I am to plant in this garden patch; and Grandfather is going to cultivate his own. He can use his methods; and I am going to let things grow naturally."

"Not entirely naturally," Tidy-up said with a hint of mischief.

"Yes. Naturally," Cassandra said to politely correct the ant.

"What I mean to say is, given that you are willing to work with us, and have elected to refrain from adding more poisons to the ground; we will work with you. I can assign my own dedicated task force to patrol your garden. No insects, apart from the Unriddables will cause you, or your crops, any trouble" Just as Sister Tee uttered the words, who should arrive on the scene but her sweetheart, R. Killies. As Cassandra gazed into the near distance she spied his pack of ready warriors waiting at attention. "Fate is being kind, Cassandra; for it appears that R.Killies has also come forward to make his troops available; should we need them." Having stated those words she gave her new beau the most seductive batting of eyelashes that any ant in the history of the world was ever known to do. "I was always told to stay away from soldiers," she admitted, "but there's something irresistible about getting to know someone so different from yourself; especially when they prompt you to look freshly at everything life has exposed you to."

With those words, Sister Tee accompanied the very charmed and equally grateful R.Killies for a private walk. Cassandra was left to ponder a number of puzzling things. She'd start with the most obvious.

"Do you know what the Unriddables are?" She asked Nutra and Tidy-up.

"Sure. Doesn't everyone?" Nutra answered.

"I'm not sure I do," Cassandra responded.

"I'm sure you do," Tidy-up responded. "Ever had a mosquito bite? Had a fly buzz in your ear, or a gnat in your eye?"

"Of course." Cassandra curtly responded.

"Well, you didn't think they were part of our circle did you? They weren't invited to Queen Buzz-bee's ball; and they're certainly not related to any of the twelve rays," Nutra said with attitude.

"Not me, Sister Tee, or any of us can really protect you against them," Tidy-up said with a note of regret in her voice.

"You see, they were never intended; but now that they're here, no one, not even your Grandfather for all his bug sprays, has a clue how to get rid of them. That's why we call them the Unriddables."

"Well how did they get here?" Cassandra asked with exasperation.

Tidy-up and Nutra whispered among themselves so inaudibly that Cassandra could scarce make out a single word. Then they began to converse with other members of the sixth ray that she had never been formerly introduced to. After convening their short impromptu conference, one spoke up.

"With respect to your question, we think that matter might best be left in the dark." Whitmore added with a touch of grave seriousness.

Cassandra, evidencing an inquisitive mind that many would say was solid proof of the laws of heredity, was hardly going to let the matter drop without a debate. "Well I think it's very impolite to bring up a subject and then leave me wondering whatever it is that you're talking about."

Her bait worked. One quality consistent with the sixth ray that left its mark on all members was a love for explanations, the desire to clearly and carefully characterize subjects, categories, explanations, and above all things!

"Perhaps you're right," Tidy-up relented. Then looking at her peers, she asked, "Would anyone care to explain?"

A tiny ant with a voice that would have better fit an elephant marched forward to provide a most profound explanation. "We refer to the dark creatures as the fallen ones; and as is plainly noted, they arise from stagnant festering waters. In those quagmires live the unhealed wounds of a great many; and what comes forth from those tainted pools is a taste for vengeance. The mosquitoes and gnats embody a leftover hunger for blood."

To Cassandra those words sounded more chilling than any horror film she'd ever seen; but she was gripped by the strange logic behind them. "Flies are not bloodsuckers, are they?"

"Not all. Mostly they prefer to be nosy busybodies, the perpetual pests that arise from the world's abundant pockets of gossip. Every time people gather round to talk manure, or speak behind others' backs, a fly is born." Pedia stepped forward to add.

"The actual colloquial expression is to talk s—t," but we prefer to edit our words for etiquette's sake. Face it: flies generally congregate in doo doo!" Nutra added.

"I see," Cassandra responded with a giggle. She certainly would have talked longer, but suddenly Grandfather began walking toward the garden. It was too late to thank them for visiting with her, or acknowledge her gratitude for their generous offer to guard her garden. She hoped they'd understand her abrupt exit.

"Cassandra! Child! It's high noon. You don't want to be outside during the heat of the day. Come on inside, let's have some lunch. We can return to the garden later, in the cool of early evening." He put his arm around his Granddaughter as he escorted her into the cottage, and then added, "For a minute there, I thought you were talking to someone."

She knew he would not believe her if she tried to explain her hard earned capacity to tune to the subtle languages of the little beings; but she also sensed in his comment a means to a desired ends.

"Grandfather, it is a little lonely out here. Can't you let Ezekiel out again?"

"He's on probation. That bird is a troublemaker!" He added with irritation.

"Well, if I helped you put wheels on his cage, couldn't we wheel him outside so he could keep me company? You could keep the key to his cage in your pocket. That would be secure, wouldn't it?"

Grandfather didn't immediately answer for he was just then considering how downright annoying it was to have an extension of his own flesh capable of outwitting him.

"Grandpa, did you hear me?" She asked eagerly.

"Let's have lunch. We have plenty of time to discuss Ezekiel's house arrest. I have not determined if yard privileges are yet feasible."

"Well, I'm partly responsible, too. Are there any chores I can do to help him regain his lost liberties?" Cassandra's vocabulary had markedly improved from her amazing encounters with so many new friends and familiars. Grandfather was impressed.

"Perhaps I can think of something," he said to placate her. He was beginning to realize that she was rather a remarkable child. And furthermore, that there was more than a hint to the adage, 'from the mouths of babes.'

However, philosophy would have to be shifted to the back burner, for it was time to place pasta on the front one! The two were ready for lunch; and it wouldn't be long before their favored dish was enhanced by fresh greens from their very own garden.

A PARADE OF VISITORS

Cassandra tended to her portion of the backyard garden as if she was a mother endlessly devoted to newborn babes. She gathered mulch mostly comprised of pine needles and rich leaf sediment to nourish the soil; and she watered. While watering, she sang to the slowly emerging plants, marveling at the way their green forms rose from the silent umber earth. The ants had diligently kept watch on her fledgling harvest, and she was grateful. In fact, she was so pleased that she made a separate little plot for her insect friends so they could partake of a complimentary harvest to their hearts' and tummies' content. (Although she was not completely sure they had hearts or tummies.) Still, it seemed this was the right thing to do. Every being was entitled to some payment for his or her services, she reasoned. She was also grateful for their company, especially since Ezekiel had not yet won his furlough, or gateway back to the great outdoors, also known as Grandfather's yard.

As had proven customary Nutra, Tidy-up and Pedia arrived as soon as Cassandra began her morning garden chores.

"You're beginning to get the hang of it," Nutra said, approving of the garden's promising new growth.

"There's a great order to things; we only need play our part. And as I so like to say, never put off doing today, what if done right might help your tomorrow!" Tidy-up added.

"And just wait till you taste what you grow! No better lesson than that! Too many human children think food comes from pretty store-bought packages," Nutra elaborated.

"I meant to ask you something," Cassandra began. "Every time I've ever been to a picnic, as soon as anyone drops crumbs, ants are right there. How do you guys do that?"

"Well, we ARE the master ray of efficiency," Pedia responded.

"But apart from that, these antennae can explain a lot. They are highly adapted for reading cues and scent signals emanating from the environment," Nutra explained.

"Yeah. Our antennae are great. They operate through twin portals that allow the best possible congruence between logic and intuition. We have sharp senses as a result," Tidy-up said with marked acuity.

"In your human brain, an adaptation has occurred that allots you twin cerebral hemispheres. Just like both of our antennae! One's for logic, and the other for intuitive also known as visionary perception. It's evidence of the great plan at work!" Pedia added.

"Except I don't smell crumbs the way you do," Cassandra offered.

"Well, we all have different gifts, you know." Then changing the subject, Tidy-up said, "Take a look at who's come to join us!"

The party suddenly noticed Beguila staring back at them from her new web, which incidentally radiated an entirely novel textural design theme.

"Is that you, Beguila?" Cassandra inquired. "Good thing I don't have any ribbons in my hair today," she said half-jokingly.

"Of course it's me. We members of the third ray thrive on short excursions. In other words, we get around! How else could we take note of the exciting developments happening in our communities? Besides, a great deal of satisfaction in life can be found in location, location, location!"

Cassandra thought the spider sounded just like a popular real estate advertisement she'd heard repeated on television. She wondered who was copying whom?

"As a baby spider I was taught that we can't always change what we get in life; but we certainly can change our perspective. A new home works wonders for my state of mind. After all, I live on the web. And let no one tell you differently, it was the third ray that posted the first websites! It wasn't those worldwide web hotshots! It's a darned shame we never obtained a patent. Heaven knows the concept is worth gazillions today!"

Cassandra was no longer intimidated by the large spider who proved quite easy to converse with. So she stood up to closely inspect the intricate web. Beguila was proud of her handiwork, and quite delighted to show it off to an appreciative admirer.

"You know it's a strange and wondrous thing. I make it a point to change my web design everyday; and sometimes as I spin the orbs, I whirl like a veritable dervish! The oddest thing about it is often the design appears to practically design itself. Seems I just come along for the ride. Honestly. It's as if my work is guided and that's how the great weave gets threaded! Alas, serendipity does favor the prepared mind. Now where did I hear that? Must've been something I collected on the wind."

Suddenly Beguila flipped over. "Go ahead and call me a breezy sort, but there is something utterly delightful about hanging upside down to air out one's thoughts. Now what was I saying? Ah, yes. Let me put it to you another way. I find that as I begin weaving my web each morning a pattern begins to unfold in a way that exceeds my expectations! It's that gift of inspiration. After all when you really think about it, true art is a collaborative process that rests upon forces unseen."

Those were profound words, not to mention concepts for a person of Cassandra's tender years. She didn't entirely understand Beguila's complicated explanation; but it would leave an imprint that would come to mean more in later years when Cassandra began to design projects of her own.

That afternoon after a pleasant lunch, Erroneous surprised Cassandra by unlocking a padlocked door at the back of his laboratory. Then he emerged with two sets of old wheels, a hammer, and some nails.

"I am pleased that you are keeping your promise and staying reasonably occupied within the confines of my ample yard. Ezekiel, I believe, has also learned from his recent exploits. Therefore if you will help me to lift and steady his cage, I believe we can come up with a way to attach these wheels. Then you can maneuver him into the yard so that he can enjoy the progress of your garden. Besides, it will give you a companion to talk to. I am not entirely ready to give up my research, although it has taken a definitive twist; so as is my habit, I will still be devoting time to the lab."

The two tinkered with the cage which inclined it to veer precipitously hither and yon. This was far from a pleasant experience for the prisoner inside; but eventually the wheels did become firmly attached. That meant the parrot now presided over a veritable caravan of his own. To say that he was relieved to get back outside would constitute a gross understatement. Ezekiel's mobility added a new flavor to Cassandra's daily garden routine. And while she still sat down for granola each morning at breakfast hour, the need to secure a key from atop the kitchen cabinet belonged to the past. Instead she got a real kick from wheeling Ezekiel outside. The innovated mechanism that facilitated the cage's maneuvers was by no means new or modern. Sometimes Cassandra took advantage of that fact and purposely teased the bird by veering his unwieldy cage over an obtrusive bump. He never got to ride a real roller coaster, she reasoned; so this would have to be his fun! Ezekiel played along. Yet when the professor was nowhere in sight, he would resume his preferred role and return to masterful tutorials. Although Cassandra never asked the parrot where he learned the facts of life, she did note that he knew a thing or two about companion planting. It required little scrutiny to realize that the sagacious bird had a vested interest in the accelerated growth of her personal berry patch. In any case, she really liked having him around. He was more than a friend, better than a guide, and existed in some category betwixt those two definitive worlds.

It was a happy day when the first blossoms opened to signal the pending arrival of fruit. Berries were about to bloom on carefully tended vines; tomatoes were showing themselves, and broccoli florets were slowly forming. The flowers attracted some bees from the Queen's royal court; and it wasn't long before the Alluras made a visit to Cassandra's garden, accompanied by an older pair of butterflies. Cassandra reached out to touch their beautiful buttery wings as a gesture of welcome.

"Please! No tactile contact. My wings are gossamer delicate; that's why I seldom go out at night. I must maintain my beauty sleep. How else could I inherit such good looks? Mother always said, 'to add beauty to the world was a noble calling,' and I believe she was right." Mrs. Allura might have been a tad more modest, if you asked Cassandra; but her husband cut in to further defend her point.

"And it was a great human philosopher who stated that beauty inspires truth. Another very good thing if you ask me," he added while gazing at his adored partner. The pair proved as adept at carrying on a conversation while fluttering their wings, as in the more elaborate art of dance. In fact, Cassandra noticed that their logical faculties were well developed, too! "Where would this world be without beauty?" He continued. "Why take a look at that lovely pattern created by the illumined shadow of leaves upon that thick tree's trunk? A great painter would struggle to do it justice, don't you think, darling?" He posed the question to Mrs. Allura.

"I think I'd like to get back to my chrysalis, dear." She answered. And then looking at Cassandra while rapidly moving her lovely wings, she added, "Everyone should have time in a chrysalis or cocoon of their own. It revives the spirit; and it's just plain wonderful to enjoy a zone built for solitude and meditation. Do you think I could dance the way I do if I didn't have a sense of balance set firm on the inside?"

Cassandra had never thought about that before.

"Besides, the chrysalis is where magic and transformation happen." When she stated those intriguing words, the elder butterfly pair danced nearer to the small flowers that were new additions to Cassandra's already inviting garden. "Let me introduce you," Mrs. Allura said, "This is Abe." Cassandra observed the elder butterfly take something of a bow in the midst of his slow and carefully executed flight routine. "And this is Bern," Mrs. Allura added. "His partner of many seasons."

"Those are strange names for butterflies," Cassandra reflexively responded, not realizing her comment might appear impudent.

"Well, you know we all go through so many changes in life," Mr. Allura qualified. "Each of us is so much more than we think ourselves to be. How can a single name capture it all? A rose by any other name would smell as sweet."

"He's quite right, dear," Mrs Allura elaborated. "And I so love when he quotes Shakespeare. Now as for me, don't forget I once had an earlier incarnation as a chubby earthbound thing; but just look at me now! Of course you could also say that beauty runs in my family."

"What my partner means is that our kind is endowed with the mysterious power of transformation; and it occurs within the quiet chambers of the chrysalis. Like the sarcophagus, it is there that each of us encounters the dream of our ancestors, who beholding themselves as weightless as air, as shimmering as light's majestic spectrum, became all that. Hence we emerge with colorful wings! A wondrous thing!"

"Almost as fulfilling as sharing life's adventure with someone who can anticipate your moves," Abe added.

"Indeed it's a wonderful life when someone complements you," Bern offered.

"We're a great team," Abe stated proudly.

"And I wouldn't have it any other way," Bern added, as the two flew off joyfully, albeit slowly together.

"It's not that we members of the seventh ray always agree on everything," Mr. Allura qualified. "We do however see fit to hone each other's game, refine each other's moves, and occasionally tweak our significant other's reasoning process. That way we opt to bring out the best in each other. Our incentive is none other than that of the helpmate ideal."

"It works like an invigorating tennis match. Perhaps you could think of it that way," Mrs. Allura elaborated further.

"You should be so lucky when the time comes to find a partner you dance truly well with," the pair intoned in near unison, as they flew off together just as the large looming figure of Grandfather approached, his shadow preceding him.

It required no rocket scientist's keen eye to recognize that Cassandra's garden patch was rapidly blooming ahead of schedule; while the professor's plants looked tired, limp and weary. He took a break from his lab routine to visit with

Cassandra. Noting the ostensible contrast he faced, he mumbled to himself, "It's the darnedest thing. How is it possible that there are no holes in her plants when she uses no sprays, while mine look lifeless? Furthermore, how is it that hers appear to be growing well without any chemical assistance?" Dismayed by the empirical data before him, he scratched his head, entered the house to check an expert text in his office library; and then returned as if in trance to head to his lab where things were always under his relished control.

Cassandra turned to Ezekiel and said, "He gets stranger all the time!" Luckily, the two had the garden all to themselves so they could freely host visits from the twelve rays. Just then making his cameo entrance into their little neck of the woods E.Z. Hopper jumped in.

"Be careful!" Cassandra yelled gently. "A landing like that could crush the new seedlings that have just begun their journeys."

"Journeys? That's an odd notion," E.Z. responded.

"Well, Radner made it perfectly clear that the seed's program is as sophisticated as any computer's. So I don't want you to jar their mechanisms. Okay?" Cassandra chided.

"Jar their mechanisms? I don't suppose Radner told you the mess he made of some hazelnuts a while back, huh? Did he bother to mention those facts"!

"Enough, you two!" Ezekiel shrieked not realizing he would be imposed upon to play the role of referee on his first fine sunny day outdoors in too long.

"I think what this girl needs is some exercise. Whaddya say, big bird?" Before Ezekiel had a chance to respond to the irreverent remark, E.Z. continued, "When's the last time you climbed a tree, huh?" His mood suddenly altered, and he got lost in his own game hardly giving either a backward glance as he jumped off to scout the yard for something very specific. It turned out to consist of toughened blades of grass. Once these were located he deftly crafted them into something of a circle; then suspended his proud sculpture from a nearby protruding tree root. He went on to collect a stack of several tiny rocks which he comically dribbled like basketballs before tossing them into his ad hoc net.

Cassandra could not take her eyes off the engaging, enterprising, athletic insect. He took notice of her noticing him and continued.

"Ever shoot hoops?" He asked. "You gotta feel free and stretch your muscles out. There's nothing like unrestricted movement to clear the mind. Then you take aim and . . ." (With those words he pretended to shoot an invisible arrow off into space) "Generally hit your target."

"That was cool. Could you do it again?" She asked, quite amazed by the insect's persuasive antics.

"Sure I can do it again. But what I really want to know is if you caught my drift?"

"I didn't know I was supposed to catch anything?" She said with arresting naivety.

"Okay, Cassandra: here's the score. I'm working my butt off to illustrate a key point by way of analogy. Because as a member in good standing of the ninth ray, it's incumbent upon me to teach what you folks refer to as the higher understanding. It all comes down to how the mind works. Okay. You dig?"

There he was, doing it again. Asking her if she dug; when it was plainly apparent that having set a garden, she knew quite well how to dig. "Yes, I dig!" She said indignantly.

"Then I'll get on with my little lecture; for I happen to know that you can make magic happen with your own mind." With those words he succeeded in getting her full attention, for what child would not wish to know more about magic? "You have to think of your thoughts as arrows. If you hold them firm and focus on where you're sending them, then they tend to reach their intended targets. In other words, if I want to become a great artist, the thought I send out is that I am a great artist. That's the bull's eye! You see I gotta see myself painting. Then I visualize others looking at the paintings that have come through my very own talented strokes. Then presto!"

"Is it really that easy?" She asked.

"Not entirely since life demands varied lessons and experiences of everyone. However, I do know that it's just as easy to direct your thoughts down a positive lane of expectancy, instead of a nasty, negative pessimistic one. Watch!" He took another one of his tiny stones and carefully aimed it toward his homemade hoop. Indeed, it passed right through the circle.

"Two points!" Offered Ezekiel, observing both the "basketball" game and Cassandra's responses to E.Z's rather admirable tutorial.

"Thanks, bird," he said offering a bow to Ezekiel. Then he returned his attention to Cassandra. "So it comes down to this: Aim your thoughts toward the outcome you desire and more often than not it'll all work out. I can't say always. Ain't no such thing as always; but I'd personally rather point my thinking in an optimistic direction, then toward the worst of possibilities. Thoughts are a form of collateral; so you got to understand what you're investing in. How about you big bird, you on my team on that one?"

"Alas, yes. Mr. Hopper. And may I say that was quite well spoken; although my position is not shall we say up for grabs." Ezekiel answered with stately poise.

Not sure what he meant by that, E. Z. hopped off again in pursuit of some device, prop or otherwise unexplained artifact. He mumbled to himself while searching the grounds, "I need some music, man. Gotta find something to make music." After jumping past the end of the professor's garden, he returned with something held tenderly under his long right arm. Cassandra could have guessed. It was a mushroom! A fresh delightful little button of a thing.

"This one's got good acoustics. I already checked." Ezekiel sat down on a stone, and then balanced the mushroom between his legs. He wasted no time in announcing his impromptu act. "Spirit's moving me, so I think I'll play a little song for you. And as a band of one, I'll be sounding off the lyrics, too. Yep, don't mind if I do."

Nothing like show-time on a lazy summer afternoon! No doubt Grandfather would be making the rounds soon enough; however Cassandra certainly had a soft spot for the amusing grasshopper. Still, in the back of her mind she wondered how Grandfather would react if he happened upon their unplanned outback talent show?

"In case our paths don't meet again, Cassandra, here's a tune to take with you."

He breathed deeply, got his rhythms going, and then began:

> "This world we share is not just meant for you
> It just so happens that it's our habitat, too.
> Nature's resources have been invaded, intrusions never stop.
> And what the heck for? To build more shops or parking lots?
> So I decided to take a poll among creatures today,
> These are my findings, what they cared to say:
> I asked the frogs as they croaked their pond songs,
> They answered that they'd noticed something's gone awfully wrong.
> The rain seldom returns to where it used to flow,
> And in other areas, flooded victims are left in a state of woe.
> He said mankind had forgotten the basic laws of harmony,
> And in full agreement responded a woodpecker, from a tall tree;
> The owl called out; then her mate responded in kind.
> He said perhaps it was not the bat, but mankind that had gone blind.
> So like my friends from the star circle, I offer you a new view
> Based on timeless lessons, we twelve rays have determined to be true.
> Let the luminous star within each
> Guide that the dangerous darkness might cease.
> And by all means do not keep what you have learned here a secret;
> Spread it about, for the world can scarcely afford to miss it!
> Imagine if we all imagined true unity . . .
> How great this world could ultimately be?"

When he finished, he stood up for a bow; while Cassandra clapped. Ezekiel sent out strange and piercing whistles of applause. Cassandra joyfully commented, "That was amazing! You really do make a good musical director!" And she would have lathered on yet more compliments to the appreciative creature, had the professor, now responding to the commotion of Ezekiel's fever pitch not done his best to run quickly their way. E.Z. slung his new drum under his arm, and diligently hopped away. He was sharp enough to locate ready camouflage and took cover under a languid leaf. He knew to avoid the professor and any uninvited sprays that might otherwise render him a not so unsuspecting Guinea Pig.

"What is it? What is it? What was so urgent that you called me out here in the hot sun? Is it lunch time yet?"

Knowing it would be of little use to tell Grandfather the truth in this case, she covered for Ezekiel. "It must be the gardening, Grandfather. I suddenly feel a little dizzy; perhaps I'm just hungry." As Erroneous placed his arm around Cassandra to guide her into the cottage, she turned to offer Ezekiel a wink.

"I suppose he'll be all right out there alone," the professor said, while placing his hand deep into his lab coat pocket to make sure that the key to Ezekiel's cage was still securely located there.

The two disappeared inside for lunch as Ezekiel practiced a number of elaborate whistle tunes of his own. The great outdoors inspired his memory bank, where old rusty songs were held like those inside a player piano waiting for someone to wind it just the right way.

THE HARVEST

Several weeks had passed and the moon was nearly full again in the sky. The professor had begun researching the natural repellants used by South American Indians, American military forces, and even modern cosmetic ladies in pursuit of a kinder more gentle pesticide. Cassandra noticed one of his books laid open on the office table. Among other things it suggested vanilla! She wondered if Grandfather had any baking supplies; for they had never once elected to make anything so tempting as brownies or apple pie in his kitchen. As she started peeking into cabinets, Grandfather arrived on the scene.

"Now you're not by chance searching for Ezekiel's cage key, are you?" He said while reaching into his pocket to show her that such a quest would remain off limits.

"Actually Grandfather, I accidentally saw your notes on the table; and since I wanted to check my garden under the lovely moon rays; I was wondering if there was something natural I could put on my skin to protect against all the mosquitoes?"

"Good thinking. So what is it that you discovered that you thought you might find in my kitchen cabinets?"

"Vanilla extract."

Erroneous got up and looked about as if trying to recover a distant memory. "You know, I do believe we did some baking around here once upon a time; and those bottles seem to last forever." He began opening drawers and looking in cabinets, until he came to the pantry where indeed, behind jars of everything else, sat a small glass container of vanilla extract as if left patiently waiting for this very occasion. While handing it over to Cassandra he added, "Let this be an experiment. I don't want your parents returning to find you burning up with West Nile Virus or some dread mosquito-carried ailment. If you find yourself bitten in spite of this natural formula, then come inside at once! Is that understood? As for me, I am too old to make myself an experiment for dangerous bugs to feast upon."

Cassandra rubbed the vanilla onto her arms; but wisely changed from shorts into long pants and socks. She had not been outside at night since Queen Buzz-bee's ball, and was absolutely delighted to still find the air alive with fireflies. One came straight towards her face, as if aiming to land right between her eyes! But it was not Elektra who spoke. Instead it was a new acquaintance. Still, Cassandra quickly found herself enchanted with the luminous creature.

"I wish I could do what you do," Cassandra said as the firefly flew confident circles around her head. "I wonder how you do it?"

"We were born to dance in the light. You could even say we ARE light dancing. That capacity is after all inborn to members of the eleventh ray! Probably has something to do with our basic operating instructions. Or maybe we remember our star origins? I suppose if we stopped to question it, the light might just go off." When Libertada uttered this highly abstract explanation, the two laughed together.

"I know my inner light for the precious key that it is. And I have to admit it; sometimes I do get a rush from giving people a bit of a charge. You can do it, too. Do you know how? You've got to possess a truly original thought of your own. Have you ever had an unmistakably novel, unique idea?"

Cassandra pondered the question, but could come up with no immediately satisfactory answer.

"You would know if you did, because you'd feel something akin to an amazed little light come on inside of your head. A spark! Think about it. Behind every true accomplishment is the bright concept that triggered it! That's what we taught the famous inventor Edison, and in no time he came up with the light bulb."

"That was you?" Cassandra asked incredulously.

"Why certainly. We provided the spark, the basic blueprint for incandescence; and well, you could say he took it from there. And ever since, people of the world have been liberated. No more prisoners of the night. They can make daylight at will; just like we do. And it's because invention happens!"

Cassandra wished there was a way she could bring that firefly to science class; or have it speak before an attentive audience for her school's Science Fair.

"Even though you may not sparkle quite the way I do, you do have a source of light waiting inside of you. In my case it's just more evident. All I have to do is blink and puff! I'm in my inspiration gear. You have your gifts and I have mine. It makes us who we are; for can you imagine how boring this world would be if there were a million "you's" in a crowd?"

Like two best friends Cassandra and the firefly laughed together. They must have been having a grand old time because their revelry attracted an unexpected visitor. The moon's rays fell upon the stately silhouette of none other than Sabius, the mantid. He arrived with a small parcel wrapped and carried under his impressive front arm. Approaching her with slow, thoughtful graceful moves he extended the tiny package to her. Her fingers graciously lowered to receive it.

"I have come to offer you a Writ of your own; and extend you an honorary membership in our great circle. Few attain such honors. All we ask is that you always remember this: it is a privilege to be here." The serious Praying Mantis added those solemn words before getting back on his way.

"He's such a solitary sort," Cassandra said to the firefly.

"True. That's because he meditates a great deal. But I prefer the social scene. It's a real turn-on to make friends and share well wishes with others," she added. "When you're open to meeting new companions, life can change. You become a pioneer of time! That's one way to shine your inner light to illumine new options. I mean life's supposed to be novel. We're all here to learn from yesterday without being bound by it. Otherwise if we just repeat the same explanations, talk to the same people, how can anything like history change? Where does progress come in?"

Now Cassandra wished she could bring the bright insect to her Social Studies class too! Barring so desirable an interview, she would instead do her best to remember every word stated. Since it was obvious that she was learning a great deal, she wondered if Ezekiel would notice any light bulbs going off inside her head?

"Here's how I see it, and let's face it, I've got a reputation for elucidation: why would anyone want to repeat yesterday, when they have a brand new canvas facing them. It's called today? So just remember that history does not have to repeat; and that everything that's ever been true, still is. However, even our own history has altered. For instance, centuries ago dragonflies were part of the eleventh ray coalition. However, they elected to break away to become free radicals; but we're still friends, since it's obvious that everything and everyone is ultimately related. Although I don't see much of Heresee anymore. I do miss him as he was such a daredevil!" No sooner were those electrifying words of explanation offered did Libertada fly off. No doubt to another exciting encounter.

Cassandra was left feeling that she had briefly conversed with a celebrity. A star! She naturally presumed that a creature as sociable as Libertada probably had a slew of parties to attend to. Funny enough the moonlight had attracted some night moths, and while her butterfly pals were nowhere to be seen, a majestic Luna moth fluttered near. She wasn't the only one to notice this rare, spellbinding creature. The ants, as promised, remained on duty to guard her garden. Thanks to the light of the moon she could make out their tiny forms, and with a little focused tuning of her mind, she could eavesdrop on the rather enticing conversation just then underway."

"If only I could dance like that," Sister Tee admitted.

"Well, you'll never know if you don't try," R. Killies added with all due respect. He placed his hand on her shoulder, and did his best to guide her; but in all honesty, she was stiff as a branch.

The Luna moth seemed to notice the conundrum, and flew closer to the ants in the hope of lifting them on the arc of her gracefully executed flight plan. She spoke in the hushed tone of a great Grandmother. "This is not a matter for analysis. Just allow the motion to seize and carry you . . . pretend you had wings." After offering her apropos advice, the beautiful winged one flew off. Cassandra reasoned that she probably had a date on a moonlit night, too.

"Just wing it!" R. Killies said trying his best to coax the shy ant out of her rigidly controlled posture. She was so accustomed to all work, no play, that actually letting loose to enjoy the occasion proved a greater challenge than her daily labors. Surprisingly the militant bully ant proved quite patient with his intended. "You know, I'm not sure you know this about me, but I've got second cousins out in California who might as well have stepped out of a Hollywood movie. They're practically costumed in red velvet. I'm telling you, if their army decided to do a kick-line, Sister, they'd do James Brown justice. Could be a little of that family rhythm rubbed off on me! Sure I've been accused of becoming my armor, making myself so hard that I only function as a machine of virtual destruction. But I've come to realize that a life that's forfeited the capacity to feel is not the life I wish to live. That's where you come in."

So greatly moved was Sister Tee by her partner's heartfelt words that she naturally began to swoon into his waiting arms, and then the real dance got underway. It's been called many things, but among the twelve rays it is best understood as THE mating dance. Cassandra had better manners then to pry further into the private affairs of others; so she wisely cast her attention elsewhere. She thought she'd poke about the garden. The vanilla extract seemed to be doing the trick. She wasn't feeling particularly itchy anywhere. Recalling that the sun is generally credited with providing the fuel that makes plants grow, Cassandra began to wonder if the moon played its own mysterious reciprocal part? For she could swear that just that afternoon there were no edible berries on her well cultivated vines; and now, under the moonlight, several ripe and ready fruits of the harvest seemed to glow as if inviting her taste buds to try them without further pause. She plucked a few and popped them one by one into her mouth. Delicioso! And her tuned ear also picked up on Ezekiel's unspoken desires; but she couldn't miss the opportunity to tease him. With berries in hand, she came close to his cage. Holding the coveted items just outside the reach of his beak she tempted and cajoled. "Now you have to say 'Polly wanna berry?' C'mon. I know you can do it."

Poor Ezekiel. It was not enough to be on house arrest. Bound and virtually gagged for all his dedicated teaching efforts; must he also succumb to humiliation? Instead of responding, he paced, changed directions, and paced again inside his cage. Was there no respect? He thought to himself.

"Okay. Here they come." Sensing she had insulted the bird when her motive was only based on humor, she dropped three blueberries inside; for at that moment, she was not altogether sure that he would not nip at her with his long bill. In the bird's mind she calculated she probably deserved as much!

It was then that Cassandra heard the telephone ring. Since it seldom did ring, Cassandra surmised that the professor's friends understood the life of solitude he preferred. No one would call to disturb him without a good reason. She didn't expect him to call her into the house.

"Time to come in, Cassandra. There is a telephone call for you." He held out the receiver and handed it to her waiting hand.

"Hello?" She listened to the speaker before responding. "Yes. Okay. Really? Then I'll pack. Yes. I'm fine; but I can't believe summer is already almost over. Okay. I'll see you then. I'm giving the phone back to Grandfather now." And she handed over its receiver.

Since her adventures began and picked up remarkable steam Cassandra didn't give much thought to ever going home again. How would she adjust? Suddenly waxing sentimental at the thought of leaving her good buddy and endless adventures behind, she went back outside and with the help of the partial moon's light, wheeled Ezekiel back into the kitchen. How would she tell him? Or was it possible that he already sensed the nature of the telephone call neither of them had yet expected?

Grandfather remained in his study so the cloak of privacy was not available. Cassandra would await a more opportune time to explain the change of plans to the intelligent bird. She walked with unmistakable sadness to her room, and began to assemble her things. She wished she'd been given at least a few more days notice. The sudden nature of her parents' pending return didn't allot her sufficient time to say goodbye to all her new companions, those delightful twelve rays. At least she had her sketchbook and journal to remind her of some of the treasured moments spent at Grandfather's cottage. It would be tough to fall asleep with a carnival of thoughts circling through her mind.

HOMECOMING

Knowing she'd have to cram a few days intentions into one, Cassandra awoke as she seldom did with the newly rising sun her silent alarm clock. By golly, she even beat Grandfather to the kitchen table. Up until there and then he'd been the official early bird of the household, although Ezekiel might beg to differ if given the chance! With scarcely any appetite, she guzzled down her cereal; then without divulging a word she began to wheel Ezekiel into the garden. The bird knew more than he let on; but he had the patience and good sense to allow the child to explain in her own place and time.

"It's not easy for me to tell you this, but I am leaving tomorrow. My parents are coming to get me." Letting out the words unleashed an apparent flood of tears. "I don't want to go," she said to Ezekiel, knowing full well the bird could not change her fate.

"There are many more things I could teach you. Perhaps you will return here next summer?" He cheerfully suggested. While she assimilated his proposition, he went into motor-mouth mode, for time was now most surely of the essence!

"Now that you have come to know the twelve rays, do you suppose that your own birth, or birth date for that matter, might prove something more than a mere accident?"

Cassandra was listening, but her feelings flooded her mind's capacity to reason. Ezekiel had faith that his words would leave an imprint, nonetheless. He would make efficacious use of this last available occasion.

"There is a fascinating congruence at work, my friend, between the advisements of your own religious prophets, and our circle of the twelve rays. For has it not been said that the lordly Jesus chose twelve disciples, and the great Patriarch Abraham founded twelve tribes? How old are you now?" The bird stopped, to interrupt himself.

"Eleven," the stunned youngster answered.

"So you're almost twelve, and they already are. Twelve that is." He let out something of a laugh, inasmuch as a parrot could laugh. Undoubtedly he did a great many things ordinary birds were not known to do. "So regarding your association with a particular ray, better thought of as a path, what do you suppose its purpose might be? Or have you yet determined which ray is your own? Once that is discovered, you might reasonably ask how it serves to benefit your particular expression of individuality. To elaborate further upon this point, I remind you that the twelve rays comprise the great circle. It is Creation's own wisdom map and fully demonstrates that you are part of it all; and it is all part of you! Interesting, yes? No single position can speak for all, nor was it intended to. Furthermore, all rays are needed for the full radiance of the whole . . . that it prove luminously true to its Source. And as an added attraction, each is THE chosen for his or her anointed purpose. Which brings me full circle, my dear. What might you conclude your own ray, or purpose to be?"

She could count on Ezekiel to present a complicated tutorial just when her mind preferred to drift elsewhere. But his deep questions purposely impeded her capacity to feel sorry for herself; and instead drew her to something like a tree perch where she could observe herself from a distance.

"I don't understand. I met the twelve rays; but I'm not sure what that has to do with me or my birthday?" She asked with a touch of impatient irritation.

"Perhaps I get ahead of myself. When exactly is your birthday, Cassandra?"

"August 9. So I dare you to get me a present," she retorted with a humorous challenge.

"Little wonder then that Queen Buzz-bee took a shine to you. Now I see why she was so eager to include you in the festivities as her royal guest and all that jazz. Why you're also a member of the fifth ray, practically her cosmic cousin!"

"To a bee?" She stammered.

"By now you ought to know that things are far more than they seem, camouflaged by surface appearances and the like. Perhaps your education is not yet complete. Therefore I will see to it that you learn more. In fact I will make it a point to design a sign-wise tutorial for your next visit. You can look forward to that most assuredly in the future!" The bird cocked his head to stroke his shoulder with his beak, as if to congratulate him self. Then he continued without missing a beat. "You know, sometimes I think we all belong foremost to the heavens, and are just visitors here. It could well be that a marvelously mysterious plan is wrought into the very theatre above. The quest to understand our spectacular stellar connections goes back thousands of years. Possibly it's an innate aspect of the human experience. Why your own ancestors beheld their earthbound status and looked up and out into the heavens. Picture in your mind if you can, a time when there were no televisions, radios, telephones or computers. Instead, there was only exquisite silence and the stars above. The wisest spent long hours gazing into the changing skies, and over time began to recognize the recurring cycles. They made note of what they observed, and refined their realizations. They discovered profound correspondences, sometimes even lifesaving ones."

By this time, Cassandra sat down, and entered into something akin to a spellbound state. She did not even greet Nutra, Tidy-up, or Pedia who were on duty, making their regular rounds about the garden and its perimeter. She hardly noticed their presence.

"Recognizing the importance of their findings and yet aware of their mortal state, they fashioned a set of stories to be passed down so that future generations would never lose the understanding they had worked so hard to gain. These stories have lasted across the ages, and are known as the fabulous myths. They explain the shifting vagaries, the very character of time; and they also happen to reveal a great deal about this mystery we call life. In fact, Sabius shared a compilation of such wisdom drawn from the Ancient Ones when he read from the writ."

"He gave me a mini-writ!" Cassandra added with pride.

"And that is not something many receive, Cassandra. Take that to heart! Now back to the subject, the Ancients left mankind with tools designed to expand awareness. While your scientists take the law of gravity for granted, they dismiss the equation great thinkers of long ago understood: In shorthand it is this: 'As above, so below.' Give that quotation some thought, my dear; for I promise it is a subject your mind will return to across the arc of your journey through this world. A journey, that may defeat some of your fondest dreams, I am afraid. For you see, my kind has lived long enough to know that this life can be a tricky business. You may live to see a dear friend betray you, a great love turn away to break your heart. Many see their fondest ambitions capsize; but do you know what you can always count upon? It is the one thing that endures: learning. That is what becomes all yours; and what you carry across this lifetime, some would even say lifetimes. So my best advice to you dear friend is to LEARN ON!"

Once he uttered that powerful piece of advice, a ladybug suddenly landed on Cassandra's arm. If E.Z. Hopper had been present, he would no doubt have fashioned something of a trumpet to make the royal messenger's clarion call clear and unmistakable, not to mention delivered with regal dignity. The ladybug had in her possession a tiny envelope not unlike those presented to the talented winners of The Golden Honey Awards. She was instructed to open it; but before reading its contents into Cassandra's waiting ear, she had this to say:

"The Queen has learned that you are leaving, dear girl, and deeply regrets the fact. However, she has commanded me to deliver this message to you." Then showing all due respect for propriety, and since the Queen did not advise that the message be shared with all present, the ladybug hopped closer to Cassandra's ear to deliver it in a whisper. "Her majesty, Queen Buzz-bee wishes to inform you that those born under the aegis of the fifth ray carry a great deal of courage in their hearts. That is a great gift. Further, she wishes to add that should you ever lose heart, you will find that in picking yourself up and finding someone or something else to love, which is to say put your heart into . . . that you will recover the remarkable spirit to start over again. The Queen also adds as a footnote, that patience is required." Having uttered the words, the ladybug promenaded down Cassandra's arm where she could once again engage the other guests and socialize.

While Cassandra took a silent moment to process the strange synchronicity underway, Ezekiel wasted no time in pointing out the most telling of analogies.

"There you have it!" The bird chirped with glee. "More evidence of the greatest story never told. You wished to understand your own ray, and a messenger arrives just in time! Kismet! Divine order abounds! Remember that each and every life is special, indeed THE CHOSEN to fulfill its own specific tasks and lessons. In the final analysis, each is appropriately gifted to suit their intended function. Therefore do not be fooled by those who would tell you there is only one RIGHT way to see or to feel or to be. Not after you have been introduced to the great star circle by yours truly, named aptly for indeed I have seen the wheel; and by extension revealed it to you! May I suggest that you give some thought to your namesake. No. I will not reveal the nature of its mystery, for as stated, the very passion to learn is a fire that must never be quelled in your mind or any other. This world will soon enough be yours to inherit; and if you look higher for meaning, you need not repeat the mistakes of your ancestors. Nothing is inevitable; what appears as such is generally the result of the same stories being told over and again, limiting minds as if they were designed to merely rotate about some unnecessarily restricted feedback loop."

"I best tell the Queen that she's been quoted and be on my way," the ladybug announced, taking her cue from Ezekiel's long elaboration on the art of bee-ing.

Some mechanism of the higher order must indeed have been working overtime, because no sooner did she fly off, and Ezekiel for the most part complete his magnificent soliloquy, did Erroneous emerge from the cottage door, stretch his arms into the wide, fresh, open air and say, "What a beautiful day! And fancy finding you out here, up and already at work so early, Cassandra. Have you had your breakfast, too?"

"Yes, Grandfather. Knowing that my parents are coming for me, I wanted to attend to my garden, and have it at its best in time for their arrival."

"Seeing that your remaining time here is scant indeed, would you care to go into town? See a movie? Stop by the farm stand? It would be considerate to do some shopping so we can offer your parents something enticing when they arrive tomorrow. What do you say?"

"I'll change my clothes, and wash off." She answered. Ezekiel breathed a sigh of despair. He wondered if he had completed to his own satisfaction Cassandra's comprehensive summer school education? There would be precious few remaining moments for the two of them to privately share.

The professor looked up at the sky and said, "I suppose this being such a nice day, we can leave Ezekiel outside while we go to town. No need to wheel him inside." And with those words the pair exited the cottage, and drove away. Ezekiel would not see them until much later. And even then, Cassandra would be so distracted with final packing and preparations that she would have little time to pay further attention to him.

When her final day at Grandfather's place of unexpected discoveries arrived, Cassandra walked about as if wearing heavy gravity boots on the moon. The summer had indeed transformed her; but in ways hardly evident to the eye. And Grandfather had also changed. Pop psychologists would explain he regained access to the lost 'child within.' Few realize how much they alter unless someone close lends their eyes or ears. So it was rather with amazement that Cassandra's parents finally drove up the long, winding driveway to encounter the professor hunched over his garden cultivating happy plants alongside his appreciative Granddaughter.

"Well, would you look at that?" Mr. Chambers said with a mixture of both gratitude and disbelief.

"I can't believe it," his wife answered as she let herself out of the car. Cassandra did not rush over to kiss either, in part because her hands were covered in soil; but also because she had matured into something of a young lady of the world, and left aspects of the precocious child shed like a cocoon of sorts.

"Just a minute, Mom and Dad. Let me wash up, then I'll kiss you." Cassandra said enthusiastically, while taking off her expert apron, tossing it over the patio chair, and then briskly walking into the cottage.

Just then Concha, hearing all the commotion, popped out from behind the kitchen wall and asked Cassandra, "Are you leaving just yet? Don't even think about leaving without saying a fond farewell to all of your roommates! Besides there's something I must share with you!"

"I'll catch you later," Cassandra said, realizing only after the words were stated that the roach might not interpret them as cordially intended. "My parents are here, and I haven't even kissed them hello yet!" She washed quickly and efficiently, changed into shorts and a clean blouse; and then rushed back outside. This time she gave both parents a deeply loving embrace. It was completely sincere, and yet it also served the purpose of the oldest public relations strategy known to history. Genuine affection could open the door to all kinds of unexpected negotiations.

"So, have you enjoyed your summer here? I really want to hear all about it." Mrs. Chambers asked.

Cassandra breathed deeply and collected her thoughts before answering. "Mom and Dad, this summer has completely changed my life!" she stated with marked seriousness. "So I want to know if I can come back next year?" Her tone changed to one of excited pleading.

"Next year? Isn't that a ways off?" Mr. Chambers responded, almost too stunned to commit to anything at the moment.

Erroneous entered the house in a most mysterious way, and soon returned with a gift hidden in his clasped hand. Opening it, the sun shone off the surface of yet another one of his prized gold coins. He handed it to Cassandra. "I owe you an apology, Granddaughter; and besides, I want you to have this gift. That night in the storm, I was so sure you were lost; but in many respects that might be said better of me. Your stay this summer has opened a door and led me to vital new pursuits." As he tapped the coin into her happy hand, he turned to Mr. Chambers. "Why she's shown me the way to a whole new approach to gardening, systematic observation, you name it. Cassandra is a scientific phenomenon all her own! And I happen to think this whole organic planting thing has a real future. As a matter of fact, I've begun serious research into more natural, nontoxic compounds for pest control. It's abundantly clear that a great many poisons have built up in our air, soil, and water. Why even our bodies. I know there's a better way and I'm bound and determined to discover it!"

"Grandpa! You've really changed!" Cassandra said with great satisfaction.

"Your daughter seems to feel that insects are our friends; and as a result of a garden experiment still underway, evidence supports her conviction that eradicating them would be both unwise not to mention a fruitless occupation. I've come to the realization that we can all learn to become better stewards of this world; and I've decided to begin that undertaking right here in this backyard garden. I've got plans for expansion."

Those sunny words opened the door to a fulfilling family reunion. Fresh berries were speckled over summer salads; and once again the quartet enjoyed a picnic in Grandfather's yard where much of the wild underbrush had been transformed into a fragrant, abundant select piece of Eden. When the dining was complete, Cassandra's father looked at his watch, and calmly said, "Well. We have a long drive ahead of us. Cassandra, it's time to get your things."

She scurried inside and collected a tiny bag, Tuke (who had long been neglected), and her suitcase. Concha must have had her ear to the wall, for she wasted no time in peering out to satisfy her own request for a cordial adieu.

"That sure looks heavy? Are you sure you need everything you're carrying?" Concha both stated and asked at the same time. "Not that I should talk. Members of the fourth ray have been known to collect a great many things; since for us it's a finder's keeper's world! But trust us, holding onto too much presents difficulties of a different sort. It's one thing to carry what's really precious; but too much will hold you back. That's what I am forever telling my children. If you spend your time carting around the past, you miss what's ahead of you, the present that is! And another word of advice, never presume to know what's behind any wall. I'd love to show you around this one."

"I really can't," Cassandra said. "I have to get going. My parents are waiting."

"Are you sure? *The Antique Road Show* has been requesting a private viewing for some time. We had to decline in their case, but we're willing to make an exception for you. After all, you are part of our circle, and we've come to know you so well. Oh, this goodbye is getting far too sentimental. Sheldon, bring me a Kleenex," The roach called out to what must have been one of her children. "I just hate to see you go. But I'll always remember you. Memories are the best, all those weightless souvenirs we can retain throughout our lives. So my wish for you is that you create fond memories to carry across yours."

Had Concha not been a roach, those words would have moved Cassandra to give her a hug. Instead, she reached down and gently tapped the roach on the back.

"That's the nicest hug a human's ever given me," Concha said, as Sheldon stood behind her observing.

"Cassandra, what's keeping you? Let's get this show on the road!" She heard her father yell with a voice that moved not only through the open cottage door, but penetrated the very walls. Suddenly LOTS of roaches peered out.

Cassandra grabbed her things and with a concerted effort, managed to open the front door taking everything outside along with her.

"Wait a minute, Dad, there's something I have to do." With those words, she placed Tuke in the garden. He would possibly pose as the worst scarecrow any vegetable patch had ever seen. Then she went over to Ezekiel's cage, and brushed back a tear. Mr. And Mrs. Chambers watched her as did Grandfather. The scene moved him more than he might have anticipated.

"You know, she's bonded with that bird all summer; and while I can't say I'm ready to part with him; birds do live exceptionally long lives. So I'd like him to go to Cassandra in the event of my leaving this world."

"Sure, Dad," Mr. Chambers comforted. "Although we trust that's a long ways off."

The bird, unable to resist the temptation the occasion warranted, and fully intending to lighten the mood said privately to Cassandra, "We educators also like to know that our dedicated efforts have been duly noted. So by all means please call 1-800-ASK-BIRD to let me know how I've been doing!"

Cassandra laughed, for by now she could sift through his sarcasm to what was really real. With genuine reluctance she added. "I have to go now. You've been a great teacher. The best. And I'll always remember. I mean I'll use what I know, and keep learning more. Besides, I hope I can come back next year!" She tapped his head as he bent down to receive the warm gesture. Then as she walked away he yielded to impulse and yelled after her, "Now put on your star and shine! That means all of you!"

"What odd words for a bird," Mrs. Chambers noted aloud. "Dad, did you teach him that?" She inquired.

"No. Must have been Cassandra," he stated not knowing what else to say. Dear Erroneous was not about to expound upon the notably profound explanation Ezekiel had recently directed his way. To this day the professor was not altogether sure he had not lost his mind as a result of that inexplicable encounter.

Cassandra smiled a virtual expanse between continents; then gave her Grandfather one of the longest hugs of modern history. She waved at Ezekiel knowing their paths would cross again, for theirs was a lifelong friendship. With resignation she climbed into the back seat of the family car. Her father placed her little suitcase in the trunk, got in, buckled up and ignited the engine. As the car moved carefully down the long driveway, she could no longer hear Ezekiel's learned words as he spoke to Grandfather with a note of solace.

"Alas, it is a rare and beautiful thing to behold a scientific mind newly enlightened." Although the Professor was partially flattered by Ezekiel's words, he sensed it was time to wheel his companion back into the kitchen. The cottage would be lonely indeed without Cassandra. The two fellas would share what they felt in common, a sense of loss.

Meanwhile Cassandra's family car progressed along its own trajectory down a very long highway. Her mother turned to ask, "Did you bring a book? Or do you want to finish your *Alice in Wonderland*?"

Cassandra gazed out the window, reflecting on the fresh memories as golden as the coins her Grandfather had given her, and answered, "No, thanks. I just went there."

"Whatever does that mean, Cassandra?"

Giving the question careful consideration, Cassandra realized that her parents would never appreciate that their daughter had attended a bona fide Queen's ball. It was equally improbable that they would understand the exercises in tunings that enabled her to speak so many languages to a great many presumed illiterate creatures. In such an instance it was determined that silence might evoke just the right kind of mystery. Who knows, it might even spur unexpected learning on the part of those driving the vehicle.

EZEKIEL'S SUPER SAVVY GUIDE
to becoming STELLAR SIGN-WISE

If you would like to share Ezekiel's latest tutorial and become stellar star wise, then just follow along. The wise bird recommends that the first thing you must master is an understanding of the twelve rays in relation to their Zodiac sign counterparts. It's quite useful at this point to know that the celestial circle was designed to operate like a vast intricate living mosaic wherein all the parts learn, change, and grow on account of their interactions with the others! In turn, each plays its role to enhance the whole. All rays are indisputably equal; and yet each is endowed with very specific gifts and related aptitudes. As you come to know more about your own ray, you may realize with surprise that in doing exactly what comes naturally, you add your part to Creation. So how can you best express your true, intrinsic spark, and shine brightly? Well, that wise endeavor begins with an understanding of the twelve rays, themselves:

The **First ray types** are usually born under the sign of Aries (March 20-April 19). They tend to jump eagerly into things that are new, inviting or exciting. They are natural pioneers, and fell restless when restrictions are applied to their lives from outside (authoritarian) sources. They live for the thrill of adventure and personal discovery; and will try almost anything once! They make excellent engineers, explorers, astronauts, and entrepreneurs of all sorts.

The **Second ray types** are usually born under the sign of Taurus (April 20-May 20). Such individuals are motivated by the joy experienced in beautiful surroundings, life's comfort, and a fulfillment known through their physical senses. Since they are often endowed with strong sensibilities, many make great chefs, artists, musicians, and even massage therapists.

The **Third ray types** are often born under the sign of Gemini (May 21-June 20). They are highly inquisitive. Such persons wish to know everything they can find out about the world (and its inhabitants) that surrounds them. Many develop keen minds and advanced communication skills. They make natural teachers, writers, computer programmers, salespersons, and publicity agents.

The **Fourth ray types** are generally born under the sign of Cancer (June 21-July 21). Their domain of preference is the home; and some excel in real estate as well as interior design. Such persons find life profoundly influenced by their family of birth, or that which occurs through marriage. Their best careers derive from their home-base, a family-owned business, or in providing domestic products.

The **Fifth ray types** usually are born under the sign of Leo (July 22-August 21). This Zodiac sign is associated with the heart; and compels its followers to pursue the truth that issues forth from that special organ-zone. Fifth ray types are very expressive, and often have a natural penchant for show business, or related forms of sharing their talents. Best careers can be found in education, self-employment, or the arts.

The **Sixth ray types** are often born under the sign of Virgo (August 22-September 21). They are naturally dedicated to service; and have as their guiding principle a wish to heal, help, organize, fix, or clean up the world . . . or other people. Many members of the sixth ray prove to be natural perfectionists who hold extremely high standards for themselves and others. Any career related to medicine, editing, or fact-finding suits the sixth ray personality best.

The **Seventh ray types** are found in the sign of Libra (September 22-October 22). Their lives are hardly complete without a satisfying partner, for this is the sign most closely associated with marriage and union on the great cosmic dial. Seventh ray types promote fairness and work hard to always understand the other person's point of view. For this reason they make wonderful diplomats, lawyers, counselors, and salespersons.

The **Eighth ray types** tend to be born under the sign of Scorpio (October 23-November 21). This mysterious realm is associated with the mythic phoenix who rebuilds itself from its own ashes. A theme of transformation marks the lives of eighth ray types. Persons drawn to this path are adept at solving mysteries. They often gravitate toward roles of: rehabilitative counselor, law enforcement personnel, detective, or medical researcher.

The **Ninth ray types** are often born under the sign of Sagittarius (November 22-December 21). Members of this ray are notably drawn to experiences designed to expand their mind and outlook; travel may figure prominently in that regard. A naturally positive thinker, the Sagittarius is frequently lucky, and does well in a variety of careers. These include: international investor, university professor, professional athlete, and stock market speculator.

The **Tenth ray types** are frequently found under the sign of Capricorn (December 22-January 20). They often assume roles as life's managers, politicians, and business authorities. It's been said that Capricorn children are born old, and learn to become youthful with time and experience! Members of this ray tend to be serious; but most take their personal ambitions and careers quite seriously. As a result of their discipline and strong sense of commitment, success is likely to meet their efforts.

The **Eleventh ray types** are often born under the sign of Aquarius (January 21-February 19). Advanced thinkers and the pioneers of tomorrow find fulfillment on this path. It marks the journey of natural inventors and innovators. The Aquarius will never follow traditions, for s/he is ultimately born to plot new trails for all of mankind to eventually follow. Best careers for Aquarius include the arts, politics, scientific research, space exploration, and public speaking.

The **Twelfth ray types** tend to be born under the sign of Pisces (February 20-March 19). They are extremely sensitive persons who instinctively recognize that all of life and its varied participants are related. Pisces is a deeply intuitive sign. It favors those who minister to the souls of the needy. This path is linked to hospitals, jails, and all types of institutions. Many talented musicians and inspired artists are born under this highly sentient ray, as are notable psychics!

Now it sometimes happens that a person will not identify (or feel any resonance) with their sun-ray, and there is a very good reason for this. Every one of us is a snapshot of the heavens at the moment of our birth. We are specks of time dressed up in all of its myriad potentials. That means that in a sense, the sky exists inside of us! Based on this theory of correspondences, we each possess a moon-ray (it tells much about our family life and our personal emotions), and a Mercury ray (it describes our style of thinking, and basic type of mindset). In addition, our Venus ray suggests both our artistic sensibilities as well as those persons we will find beautiful and magnetically attractive. (If individuals did not own distinct Venus positions, then everyone would fall in love with the same person!) And our Mars ray suggests the ways we will act in order to acquire, achieve or attain our personal desires. The Mars ray also describes whether we will be aggressive or passive. It points to our natural allies and foes! All this indeed proves the stuff that cosmic chemistry is made of! According to astrological theory, the sun, moon, Mercury, Mars and Venus all work like a gigantic puzzle to express the individual's personality; but the outer planets: Jupiter, Saturn, Uranus, Neptune and Pluto point to trends that are shared by an entire peer group or generation pool. There are many books on this intriguing subject; but they go way beyond what Ezekiel's tutorial was designed to teach. Of course now that the Divine curriculum has been introduced to you, you can freely pursue your own further learning! So remember, each of you is a prism of time crystallized for a unique purpose. You are here to play your own star'ring role!

In closing, Ezekiel would like to remind readers (and new students) that as a winged messenger, he functions as a natural emissary of the legendary Mercury, who according to mythology was destined to relay messages between "the gods" and the mortals of earth. The astrologer sees in the stories of myth a correspondence with the timeless functions allotted to the planets in our solar system. They act a lot like ambassadors set by Creator into the heavenly clocks-works to fulfill intended purposes; but that is a long story; and Ezekiel must now bid you adieu. He thanks you in advance for fulfilling your role in the great circle!

VOCABULARY LIST SUPPLEMENTAL GUIDE

A:

Abhorrent: distasteful
Accoutrements: tools, equipment
Accrued: to add to, to increase
Acknowledging: making note of
Acuity: keenness
Adaptation: to change, to better adjust to circumstance
Adhered: held to, attached
Ad hoc: for this case only
Adieu: goodbye
Admonishing: of a warning nature
Aesthetics: to do with beauty
Align: to line up, or bring into agreement
Alluring: irresistible
Ambiance: atmosphere, environment
Ample: more than enough
Anomaly: exception
Anticipated: hoped for, awaited
Appeasing: to give into demands
Apportioned: to divide and distribute
Apprise: to inform
Arbitrarily: action done on a whim
Aromatic: having a scent (usually pleasant)
Array: an orderly grouping
Articulation: what is spoken

Assertion: strongly expressed statement
Assessments: conditions as measured
Attire: clothing
Attributing: a quality that contributes to an effect
Audible: able to be heard
Aura: an invisible atmosphere said to exist around living beings
Authoritatively: spoken of done with authority

B:

Basso profundo: uttered in a low bass voice
Bedazzled: surprisingly stunned
Benefactor: generous sponsor
Bewilderment: sense of being puzzled
Bio-locomote (author's * poetic license) maneuver via self-generated air fuel
Bona fide: honest, in good faith
Boundless: wide, open expanse without apparent limits
Bountiful: abundant plentitude
Bristling: to stiffen with fear (or be ready to explode!)

C:

Cacophonous: loud, random sounds that don't blend
Cadence: the rhythm of a thing's execution or expression
Calisthenics: organized exercises
Captive: held as prisoner
Cerebration: deep thinking
Choreography: directed dance movements
Chutzpah: daring, showing nerve
Clandestine: mysterious or secretive, hidden
Cogitation: thoughtful meditation
Coiffure: hairstyle
Collaborative: done along with others
Colloquial: phrases used in everyday conversations
Commencement: beginning ceremony or address
Compelling: highly attractive and appealing
Compensate: to make up for, create fair balance
Competence: capacity, ability
Composure: calm self-possession

Concoctions: odd combinations
Conducive: helpful toward
Congruence: things in agreement or harmony
Conjecture: guess, inference
Conscientious: done with full awareness and honesty
Conservationist: One who uses nature's resources wisely and prudently
Conspicuously: obviously
Constituents: ingredients, parts of the whole
Contemplated: Considered after due thought
Contention: conclusion one argues to maintain (in debate)
Contradicted: to say something opposite to what had been stated
Contrivance: an invention or mechanical device
Cosmic: that which relates to the expanse of the universe
Countenance: the face or to face
Counterintuitive: self-evident
Covert: hidden, secret
Coveted: very much desired
Criteria: the standard by which something is judged
Critically acclaimed: hailed as highly talented, well-rated
Cultivate: technique to make things grow
Curriculum: teacher's lesson plan
Customary: the usual way things are done
Cynicism: lacking in faith or belief

D:

Deductions: arriving at conclusions (usually based on evidence studied)
Deftly: skillfully executed
Deliberating: considering
Delineated: spelled out
Demeanor: bearing, personality
Demolishing: act of destroying
Detainee: one held for questioning, a prisoner
Deterrent: that intended to keep others from doing something
Detritus: debris, waste
Dialects: different variations on a language (or languages) spoken
Diatribe: a learned discussion
Didactic: designed to teach something
Dignitary: individual possessed of a high status

Dilemma: problem
Diligent: Done with careful focus and determination
Disabuse: to rid of false ideas and notions
Disarray: thrown out of order
Discerned: able to recognize
Disclaimer: that which is done to deny officially
Discrepancies: mistakes, inconsistencies
Disingenuous: less than honest, falsely presented
Diversion: That which distracts attention or focus
Diversity: composed of many varied elements
Divulged: to make publicly known
Doctrine: something taught and believed to represent sound principles
Domicile: one's home or homeland
Dominion: the power to rule, or under a specific (national) rule
Du jour: (French for) regarding today

E:

Eccentricities: peculiarities of behavior and expression
Ecologists: Those committed to using natural resources in a sound manner
Elaborate: to explain in detail
Elicited: to draw out data or information
Elocution: a style of manner of speaking
Eloquently: spoken in a very learned manner
Emanating: that which is emitted from a source
Embedded: that which is firmly set into hits surroundings
Embryonic: related to the human (or other) embryo or birth origin
Emissary: one sent on a (sometimes secret) mission
Empathy: the capacity to feel what another feels
Empirical: data derived from observation and experimentation
Endorsement: recommendation
Endowed: that which is provided or given
Ensnare: to capture
Entail: to involve or include
Enthralled: captivated by
Enticing: very tempting
Entomologist: one given to the scientific study of insect and their behavior
Entourage: a group of attendants

Environs: where a thing lives
Erudite: learned
Esteemed: highly regarded
Exigency: a situation that calls for immediate action
Expedite: to efficiently make happen
Exuded: discharged, radiated

F:

Fabricating: constructing (sometimes for one's own ends)
Facilitates: to assist in making something happen
Fastidious: oversensitive to managing details
Feisty: high-strung personality
Fledgling: new and inexperienced
Finesse: using subtle diplomatic skills to handle a situation
Fixated: attention overly focused on one thing
Foliage: varied forms of plant life
Foreboding: scary, pointing to something terrifying
Formidable: a powerful challenge
Fortuitous: more than accidental
Furlough: leave of absence that is granted

G:

Garnered: collected, stored up
Gibberish: nonsense language or ideas expressed
Glitch: unexpected mistake or change in operations
Gourd: dried out hollow seeds left from a fruit

H:

Hablar Espanol: Spanish for "do you speak Spanish?"
Herbalists: those who use special plants in a medicinal capacity
Herbicides: Chemicals industrially designed to kill plants
Heirlooms: precious objects passed down from one generation to another
Hyperbole: exaggerated statement or example
Hypothetically: supposedly, theoretically

I:

Illumined: to light up or add light to
Illustrious: distinguished
Immersion: placed fully into (usually in reference to water)
Impassioned: showing strong feelings
Impeccable: perfect, without any mistakes
Impediment: obstacle, block or hindrance
Imperative: necessary
Implications: conclusions the facts lead toward
Implore: to plead
Improbable: highly unlikely
Impromptu: unplanned, spontaneous
Impudent: without any consideration for consequences
Inadvertently: accidentally, by mistake
Inanimate: lifeless, dull
Inaudible: not able to be heard
Incandescence: that which holds the quality of shining brilliantly
Incentive: compelling reason to do something
Incessantly: without ever ceasing
Incited: to urge to action, or stir up
Inclement: rough, unfavorable
Incomprehensibly: beyond understanding
Incongruent: not appropriate, things not fitting together
Incontestable: certain, beyond doubt
Incredulously: doubtful, showing disbelief
Incumbent (upon): existing of a duty or obligation
Indictment: to bring formal charges against (one presumed guilty of something)
Infused: filled, pervaded
Inevitable: bound to happen
Inexplicable: unable to be explained
Inopportune: happening at a bad time
Inordinately: excessively
Inquisitive: curious
Irreverently: without showing any respect
Interlopers: meddlers, intruders
Interrogation: formal questioning, usually by police-type figures
Intimation: suggestion, hint

Intriguing: fascinating
Invoking: summoning, calling forward

K:

Kabuki: Japanese silent theatre, mostly done in mime
Kismet: fate operating behind the scenes to make things happen

L:

Laissez-Faire: French word that means "with hands off," to just let things occur
Lethal: deadly
Linear: that which follows in a line
Logarithm: a mathematical formula for raising sums by specific intervals
Ludicrous: ridiculous (or funny)
Luminous: bright, lit

M:

Mandatory: required
Mantra: special phrase stated to supposedly invoke religious feelings
Masterminding: expert planning of a project or set goal
Mechanisms: the working parts of a system
Mesmerized: hypnotized, to hold others attention spellbound
Millennia: periods consisting of thousands of years
Misgivings: questions and doubts
Morale: mental spirit of courage and confidence
Moxie: unusually high level of self-confidence

N:

Neutralize: to balance or counteract
Nonchalant: without notice or concern
Non-partisan: holding allegiance to neither U.S. political party
Nonsectarian: Not confined to any specific religion
Notable: worthy of note
Nuances: small facets that are varied in quality or composition

O:

Obligatory: required, an obligation
Obscured: not easily perceived, vague or hidden
Obtrusive: standing out
Ominous: threatening, omen of a menace
Organic: consisting of natural ingredients
Oriented: set towards
Orthodox: conventional, traditional application
Ostensibly: clearly, obviously

P:

Palpable: easily perceived, tangible
Panorama: full landscape
Parables: short stories that evidence important moral lessons
Paradigm: a pattern or existing example
Paradox: something that holds contradictory qualities
Parlance: a style or manner of speaking
Pensive: deeply thoughtful
Perfunctory: quickly done away with (or completed without much care)
Perilous: dangerous
Permeating: penetrating and spreading throughout
Persistently: to remain on course without giving up
Pertinent: relevant, and to the point
Phenomenon: an unusual fact, circumstance, or event
Physicist: scientist who studies atoms (matter) and the laws of physics
Picturesque: pretty as a picture
Placate: to quiet another's anger, to appease
Plaintive: pleading, sad
Poignant: piercing to ones feelings (painful)
Plausibility: believability
Portrayed: to depict or to exhibit
Preconceived: opinion held before it's exposed to evidence
Precursor: the things that comes before, a forerunner
Preservatives: chemicals added to food to extend their "shelf life."
Privy: to know by way of a confidential source
Probing: seeking or investigating
Proliferate: to grow by multiplying new parts

Prologue: An introduction to a poem, play (or event)
Pronouncement: a formal statement of fact
Prospect: possibility faced
Prudent: very careful, cautious with respect to action

Q:

Quipped: replied with sarcasm and wit

R:

Rastafarian: group of individuals who wear matted hair and are found in Jamaica
Ravenous: greedy, voracious appetite
Receptivity: being open to, able to receive
Reciprocally: done in exchange
Reflexive: instinctive response
Refuge: a place of safety
Regimen: regulated system of activities or exercises
Rejuvenate: to coax life back into
Relish: to highly regard
Reminiscent: that which recalls, reminds of something past
Renaissance: period that spanned the 14th-16th centuries that celebrated art & culture
Rendition: performance in a theatrical role
Renegade: one who abandons former loyalties or a position held
Repertoire: stock of available standard performance possibilities
Replicate: to repeat results
Residue: remainder, left-over parts
Resolute: firm in purpose
Reticence: with hesitation or reserve
Revelry: noisy merrymaking
Reverberating: a sound that continues to echo
Reveries: dreamy, fanciful daydreams
Rhapsody: enthusiastic utterance, poem or song
Rhetorically: Spoken without any intention of receiving an answer
Robust: strong, muscular
Rudimentary: basic design (still under development)
Rummage: to search through vigorously

S:

Sagacious: endowed with much wisdom
Sanctuary: safe place (sometimes a holy zone)
Sarcophagus: private tombs that were made to preserve Egypt's mummies
Sauntered: walk aimlessly
Savored: ate with pleasure
Savvy: one naturally in the know, or smart
Scintillating: sparkling brilliantly
Scion: a descendant (of)
Scrupulously: very carefully and properly executed
Scrutinizing: examining very closely
Serendipity: by what appears as mere accident, but suggests something more
Sensibilities: capacity to respond through the senses
Shrouded: covered or wrapped in (implying to hide)
Simulated: to seem just like
Simultaneously: two events happening at the same exact time
Skepticism: being unconvinced, wanting proof
Solemnity: a solemn feeling
Solemnly: done with respect for sacredness (or religious ritual)
Soliloquy: lines spoken by a character in drama to reveal his thoughts
Staggered: moving unsteadily
Stamina: ability to withstand exhaustion and keep going
Stature: ones status or position
Steward: the person put in charge of supplies
Strategic: making use of sophisticated planning (often in reference to military)
Strobe: pulsing light
Sublime: beautiful and pleasing to the senses
Subtlety: a fine line that marks a distinction
Subtly: not done in an obvious manner
Succession: following in an orderly sequence
Succumbing: giving in, surrendering ones will
Summit: mountain top
Surmise: an inconclusive opinion
Symmetry: symmetry of form on both sides
Synchronicity: Believed to be unrelated events that intersect to suggest a mysterious process of relatedness

T:

Tactile: what is tangible or what pertains to touch
Tendrils: a threadlike extension of a plant
Tentatively: something done as a trial, without a commitment
Toxic: highly poisonous and harmful
Transfixed: The state where ones attention is held. They are immobilized.
Transgressions: mistakes or violations
Trepidation: fear and worry
Troupe: group of performers
Turbulence: condition of disorder and chaos
Tutelage: private education, schooling

U:

Unabashed: bold, not easily embarrassed
Unbeknownst: not known
Uncanny: ever so strange and unusual
Unimpeachable: stating what cannot be doubted or discredited
Unimpeded: able to move freely
Unremitting: not stopping or taking a break, persistent
Unwarranted: Not called for, unnecessary
Upended: to stand on end (or overturn)
Uttered: to have said

V:

Vantage point: a favorable advantageous lookout
Vertigo: A fear of heights
Vigorously: Characterized by the output of much strength
Virtuoso: one who is very talented, and/or has great artistic good taste
Visualizing: to see clearly in ones mind's eye

Z:

Zeal: abundant enthusiasm

SIOUX ROSE

The Author and Her Vision

I became interested in astrology during my teen years. Later in college I read up on the topic and began doing informal readings, i.e. chart interpretations. Privileged to study in London for one semester, I integrated courses in photography, Shakespeare, and women's studies with a private tutorial on astrology. Once graduated, fate drew me to the Caribbean island of Puerto Rico where my freelance astrology columns were featured by *The San Juan Star, Caribbean Business*, San Juan Cable TV guide, and later for prestigious glossies, *Imagen* and *Buena Vida*. My features were also published in the in-flight magazines of Capital and Arrow Airlines.

Once I became a mother, I began writing children's stories to amuse my own daughters. It wasn't until many years later that I found the perfect nest in which to "birth" *Cassandra's Tale*, the story I believe I was born to write! A lucrative contract with *Lear's Magazine* arrived when I moved to Key West, Florida to host one of the nation's only live cable television programs devoted to this intriguing subject matter. *Astrology and the Divine Order* aired across the Florida Keys to an enthusiastic audience from 1986-1994. It was during this favorable career interval that I approached New York literary agents with my idea for a higher peace model utilizing the great heavenly circle to demonstrate unity based upon purposeful diversity. I was told, "Astrology isn't for children. Besides, it's never been done!" In my view children were daily bombarded with sexual as well as violent imagery, so a taboo against looking up for meaning surprised me. Having taught junior high students (speech, English, and creative writing) I noted enthusiasm for this subject matter. Further, I was convinced that acquainting students with the twelve archetypal expressions presented a distinct improvement over both standard education and its presumed one size fits all approach. Determined to prove the

145

agent wrong, I went to bookstores and libraries on an ad hoc reconnaissance mission of my own. Sure enough I found a set of books done in England that used comic book sketches to depict the qualities of the zodiac signs. When I returned to the skeptical agent with my find, she entirely reversed herself to say, "You see. It's *been* done!"

Undaunted, I at last came to the right time and place to focus on *Cassandra's Tale*. It's been made clear to me as a writer that specific topics warrant our interest at different points in our lives. This process is quite organic. So as I headed up to Athens, Georgia (June, 2005) along the always too-hot I-75 interstate, and by the time I arrived at my hostess's home, I was utterly exhausted. She had a big surprise in store, however. Sixties phenomena Ritchie Havens was about to perform at a small, intimate downtown Athens theater. We headed over. As fate would have it, Ritchie sang a song that began with these words, "There is a great secret to life . . . that there are only twelve of us; and they are: Aries, Taurus, Gemini . . ." Since I take signs and omens seriously, I knew Ritchie's song was my clarion call to pen *Cassandra's Tale*. During its execution I unquestionably felt I had had help from higher guides in writing the story. Its sequel is already in development. And while it is my dream to see *Cassandra's Tale* become an animated film viewed by children around the globe, I am happy that this book has found its way to your hands! Championing the great circle, *Cassandra's Tale* teaches the important truth that there really are no sides.

To obtain copies of this book (and its anticipated sequel), please go either to my personal website: *www.siouxrose.com*; or to publisher, xLibris.com.